Motivation III:
The Exit

by

Swift

R H Publishing, LLC
P.O. Box 11642
Milwaukee, WI 53211

All R H titles, imprints, and distributed lines are available at special quantity discounts for bulk purchases for sales promotion, premiums, fund-raising, educational, or instructional use.

Special book excerpts or customized printings can also be created to fit specific needs. For details, write to: R H Publishing, P.O.Box11642, Milwaukee, WI 53211 or email us at talk2us@rhpublishings.com .
Visit our website @ www.swiftnovels.com

First Printing: March 2016
10 9 8 7 6 5 4 3 2 1

1. Urban 2. Fiction

Printed in the United States of America

Acknowledgements

I'd like to take this moment to acknowledge each and every supporter of the Motivation book series. Constructing this series has been an exciting journey for me. And you (the readers) have given me much motivation through this entire process. From the feedback to the support and love you've shown me at book signings, social media interaction, word-of-mouth promotion, etc., I would like to thank you all for the inspiration to continue on writing and completing this series. You're the best!!

BOOK ONE

Chapter 1 ~ Never Show Weakness

Keyshawn Watson sat silently in his federal holding cell, knowing that no matter what happened at this point, the punk-ass Feds wouldn't break him or T.A. He felt both of them were two of the toughest niggas who had ever played the game, and to their credit, they both played it strictly by the rules.

Resting his head on the steel tabletop that adorned the solid brick wall of the cell, Keyshawn nodded for a minute in deep concentration. He thought about his life for a moment, going all the way back in his past to the first day he'd met the nigga Red at the corner store on Atkinson. At first sight, he'd known Red had game about himself and Keyshawn wasn't a hater at all. Befriending Red was a must, even though he had showed Keyshawn up on their first encounter. Key opened his eyes and smiled at his brother's memory, thinking now how two young potato chip thieves made the transformation from ping-pong to pimping whores.

Key thought about his first real down hoe, how in the beginning all he was after was a piece of ass and a good time with the slick-mouth cutie pie he'd met leaving his mom's crib. It was all-good until Keyshawn found out the true identity of the girl named Quesha. Since then they had been through it all together—the good, the bad, and the ugly. Once Quesha had conformed and accepted the P from a real pimp, she'd instantly left her sucka in the wind to begin a life with Keyshawn. They wasted no time making power moves, and together they'd even tasted the vainglorious lifestyle of the hood rich and famous. Keyshawn truly missed Quesha. He touched the tattoo on his body of the Q, the ink represented gone but not forgotten.

Her knocking another hoe while out on a mission to get his money further instilled the lust for being a pimp inside him. Keyshawn knew that was the way the game was sometime played. When your shit was game-tight, your bottom-bitch's mission wasn't only to get money, but to be on the lookout for a wife-in-law who could enhance the family's income. His bottom-bitch Quesha had it all: the heart, the looks, and the tenacity to always hold down the throne as the bottom bitch. He knew in his heart Venus was next in line. Keyshawn was just glad he didn't have to let the words leave his mouth about her position. Venus had done what was necessary and stepped to the plate. It would have hurt for him to verbally express it, but if the bitch needed confirmation, he would have had to do it.

The door opened to his cell and Keyshawn expected to see another one of them fag-ass prosecutors heading through the walkway in attempts to break him or offer some kind of plea deal that the average Joe blow would have taken. He thought about Big Daddy's words when he spoke on the percentage of niggas who copped out when those people had them in their grasp, making it seem like they were indestructible agents of the law.

"Fuck that!" he spat out to himself.

Key knew his strong pimping put a serious damper on a lot of things for the Feds. He also knew they didn't have exactly what they thought they did. Surely if they were attempting a second chance at turning him into a statistic, they could do what he'd asked and just turn right back around and speak with his attorney. He was one hundred and didn't have shit to say to the police. Keyshawn knew T.A.'s mind was on the same thought process as well. They were tighter than Chinese eyelids, and one thing for sure, as two thugs were certain, they could count on each other and count on having each other's back.

Keyshawn looked at the figure who emerged and was staring his lawyer in the face. He didn't like the anguished look his hired gun bore as he walked in. Sweat poured from his bulbous nose and the frustration was clear to Keyshawn. Keyshawn's lawyer looked at the guard eyeing him. The federal agent left the two alone because, by law, attorney-client meetings were still privileged, even during booking. Keyshawn waited for the police officer to vacate before speaking.

"What's up, man? What's the sad face for?" Keyshawn asked.

His attorney didn't answer; instead he opened his leather, two-thousand-dollar Louis Vuitton briefcase and removed a handheld portable television. It was already powered on and the volume had been turned all the way down. This is what the lawyer intended as Keyshawn sat there in disbelief, reading the closed caption.

The camera crew was catching everything on tape as hundreds of Feds surrounded his homie Tiahmo's crib. He knew this couldn't be good for him and T.A. if Tiahmo got charged with the murder of a federal agent. He glared closely at the small three-inch screen and noticed his baby-mama on the scene in full work garb, wearing her FBI jacket with a bulletproof vest under it for protection. Keyshawn had put his all and last hopes into Kimmie. So far, she'd been coming through for him, but as he saw what was transpiring now, he wasn't quite sure how this new episode was going to work out.

"Turn it off!" Keyshawn demanded, not wanting to get overemotional. "What the fuck you showing me this for?" he asked hastily.

Keyshawn was wise to the streets and to the game, maybe even wiser than the allotted time he'd spent in them. He knew, even though he'd paid this white man top dollar to defend him, at the end of the day, this same motherfucker was going to be talking about him behind his back Sunday afternoons on the front nine. *And* with the very people who were against him, prosecuting him, trying to send him to some correctional facility for the rest of his life.

"I just hope this doesn't come back to bite us in the ass," his attorney said, choosing his words and tone carefully. "If it does, Mr. Watson, you're probably going to need to wake up my comrade Johnny Cochran, because I can assure you, they will do anything in their power to hand you and your friend the death sentence," his attorney exclaimed with a hint of finality behind his tone.

Just the mention of the death penalty shook Keyshawn up for a second. His thoughts traveled to the last phone call he'd had with his mother. His father was dying and now maybe he would be joining his old man on the other side of the clouds.

"Listen suit," Keyshawn said, not calling his attorney by his government name, "that shit there don't got shit to do with me. Now do you have any news on what this grand jury is plotting on a nigga's future?" All the time he was wondering every second of Tiahmo's outcome.

"It seems they are stalling for some reason. I'm not sure what the reason may be, but a case of this magnitude and charges like they assessed, I don't see them stalling as an advantage for the home team," his attorney said.

Keyshawn knew exactly why their dumb asses were stalling. A small smile creased the corner of his lips as he thought about all the work his bitch had put in. The government's case was mangled: their strongest evidence was in shambles and the so-called witnesses they thought they would have weren't cooperating. He knew it would be awfully hard to convict a man of any charges with no evidence and no cooperation.

"I'm not going to jump to any conclusions, Mr. Watson, just yet, but it's a good thing they didn't break any of your girlfriends.

Otherwise, we would be in front of a grand jury right now, but your friend might not be so lucky."

"Not so lucky? What the fuck's that shit supposed to mean?" Keyshawn asked, knowing Apple and T.A's other piece had held fast like all the girls had done. It was almost impossible to believe he and T.A. both had stables of down-bitches who were riders for their pimps.

"They got to somebody named Natalie who was an acquaintance of his, and she gave up any and all information she could."

Keyshawn was trying to recollect the name, but it wasn't coming to him at the moment as he racked his brain to search for the familiarity.

"Okay, Mr. Watson, I think I'll go home until they call me. When they do, trust and believe I'll be ready," his lawyer said and walked out.

Keyshawn sat there thinking about the scene he'd seen on the television screen. It was the first time he'd actually worried about Li and the safety of her life and his unborn child. He thought again about his father and how Tim had left him and his sister to either be raised by another man or the streets, and was uncertain if that's what he wanted to do. In his whole career as a pimp, this was the second time Keyshawn could ever remember being uncertain.

He thought about McComb and wondered if he had stayed down there, would he be in college now on his way to becoming a doctor or a lawyer himself? That was something every mother said when she gave birth to a child, "This is the next doctor or the next president of the United States," as she held her baby in their arms, all the time knowing, as soon as they left the hospital, most mothers were headed back to a life of struggling and wondering how-in-the-fuck they were even going to feed the so-called doctor or president. The closest president who'd had any ghetto experience was Clinton.

Keyshawn thought about his grandmother and knew by now she'd gotten the news her favorite grandchild was in the slammer facing some serious time. He thought about the last time he was there after leaving New Orleans and how bad he wanted to help her bake his favorite cake. "Take them girls home and make sure they get some rest. They's tired now," were her last words.

That's when it had dawned on him who this Natalie was. He remembered having a pimp talk with T.A. one day about sometime having to let a bad bitch go no matter what her accomplishments were. T.A. had told him one monkey don't spoil the show and Natalie, Natty as he called her, was a cold monkey but had gone too far. He had dismissed her, sending her out of town with a few peanuts and her walking papers. He said the bitch wanted revenge, but she had ceased when his stable had beat the shit out of her.

Keyshawn put his head down on the table, knowing he possibly couldn't save T.A. because neither of them had had any idea Natty had resurfaced. Keyshawn had a quick thought about Paris and he wondered why his brother had even let Natty breathe another breath after her first stunt.

Chapter 2 ~ What's Love Got To Do With It

Li Chan stood behind the black unmarked Chevy suburban next to her boss SAIC Bender. He had just finished commanding the suspect inside to come out and surrender peacefully. Bender felt the resistance the perp was putting up wasn't just because he was inside the dwelling thinking he was being hassled for a simple probation violation. He felt this type of behavior displayed an insurmountable realm of guilt on the man inside. Bender knew now he had his man—one of the people responsible for killing Agent Daley was barricaded inside. He still wanted to stick to the primary plan to take this guy alive, remembering the young couple who'd come forward had seen what happened. They both said there were four members in the van handling Daley's corpse.

"Boss, doesn't look like he's going to come out on his own," Li said, hoping from the bottom of her heart, knowing the man inside was Tiahmo, that he wouldn't willfully surrender. Her whole life flashed in front of her thinking about the story he could tell to save his own ass. If that happened, not only was she going to be a disgrace to her family for the child who was steadily growing inside her, but she had been party to the murder of a government law official, and even worse, her own partner. Li Chan knew she was surely going to the chair or to the gas chamber if her team apprehended Tiahmo.

"I didn't think it was going to be this easy," Bender replied.

"That's the van in the driveway," one of the agents said.

"Yeah, I know. I bet that time of night these people had no idea they were being watch by a couple of suburban miscreants looking to roll in the hay," Bender replied.

Li Chan was glad she'd never touched the van.

Now it made a little more sense to Li Chan. She had wondered how the department had gotten the drop on Tiahmo and his crew in less than twenty-four hours. Her first thought was Daley had an accomplice helping him she didn't know anything about—maybe a close friend or family member he'd let in on the plan, and they'd witnessed his execution. That notion vanished when she heard Bender mention the two witnesses who'd seen the whole burial take place. *'Talking about being in the wrong place at the wrong time,'* she thought silently.

"I don't think we have a chance here at this being peaceful, boss. If the man inside knows we're here about a murder, he's going to do everything in his power to get away," Li said irritably.

"You know, Chan, I think you're right. Besides that, it's going to be hard to stop these boys from taking a kill-shot. Daley was one of our best!" Bender exclaimed, taking the bullhorn from someone.

"He lost his first wife because she made him choose between the job and the marriage. I guess it's obvious what he chose," Bender continued, making a statement more so than asking Li Chan a question.

Li had no idea her partner had been married before. Daley had always been making eyes at her even though he'd never tried anything. It was strange he'd never talked about a wife or any other woman, period. She knew he'd secretly had a crush on her but wouldn't act on it, which was her assumption of why he hadn't turned her in from the jump. She figured the money he wanted was just the first step to his bribery.

"I have an idea, boss. I still have a rep with these guys as being Kimmie. Why don't you let me get back to my undercover performance and go in there on this guy?" Li said, not knowing Tiahmo had seen her in the Fed jacket from the second story window.

Li also had been oblivious to the fact that when Keyshawn and T.A. had hired Tiahmo, they hadn't briefed Tiahmo on her double-crossing involvement. Tiahmo hadn't the slightest idea the woman he was seeing outside was actually there protecting Keyshawn. Li was willing to put herself in grave danger to protect Keyshawn, but one thing she wasn't willing to do was give birth to her child in some women's federal correctional facility.

"Wait a fucking minute, Chan!" Bender said, back to chorusing his four letter words again. "What makes you think this has something to do with the Watson-Smith case?" he asked as he continued with a confused look plastered on his mug.

"I've heard the suspect's name thrown around several times when I was in the room with Smith, boss, and I remember one day Smith said he had a meeting with him."

"So you're telling me Watson and this other guy may have had something to do with placing a hit on Daley?" he asked.

"I'm not saying that for sure, but I know I recognized the name. It just took me a minute to place it," she said, covering again for Keyshawn.

"It's a long shot, boss, but what other choice do we have? I remember, we don't negotiate," she continued, smiling but serious as a heart attack.

SAIC Bender thought about what Li was asking him to allow her to do. He had to admit she had been successful thus far at her undercover assignment. The only mishap was her getting a little ill at the Grand Jury hearing, which no one could fault her for. Bender knew she was the only one who had really been on the inside with these crazy criminals, and Li also had the special training that would allow her to take care of herself if things got ugly.

Special Agent Li Chan was born in Japan, where as a child, she studied various techniques of martial arts. She was capable of handling a lot of situations that some of the men in the agency couldn't even handle. Bender was just reluctant at first because he didn't really know if the tie-in to the Watson-Smith case was valid, and if something happened to another one of his people, instead of a promotion, it would be more like desk duty. He would find himself surfing online for child predators and religious cult crimes. Bender knew he wasn't ready to go there.

"Listen, Li, there is a lot riding on the line here. If I send you in there and shit goes wrong, it could be my ass," Bender carefully explained.

"I understand, but if everything goes right . . ."

She stopped right there to let him ponder the outcome of bringing Daley's killer to justice. Bender thought about what Li was getting at a little more and knew exactly where she was going with it. They scanned the house again, using the special infra-red system that picked up the movement of only one body.

"Boss, looks like this dude is purged on the second level of the house. There is no other movement beside what appears to be an animal of some sort," one of the agents radioed to Bender from a crime-unit van parked closer to the home.

That call gave Li something extra to shoot at her boss. "Besides that he's on the second level. I won't go up if I feel there's any danger or I get a feeling my hunch is wrong," she explained.

Li knew once she got inside with Tiahmo, she'd get a chance to talk to him. She figured she could talk him into giving up because she would reveal the fact that all her people had were some teenagers who'd seen some shadows in the night. Li didn't know how smart Tiahmo was, but if she could convince him into believing, if he had an alibi for his whereabouts that night, then anybody could have borrowed his van would be his defense.

She knew it was risky talking to a man as dangerous and street-savvy as Tiahmo, but it was a chance she had to go for. Besides that, she knew if she got a chance to take the kill-shot, Tiahmo never had to worry about seeing the inside of a courtroom anyway. It was a win-win situation for her and Keyshawn. Li added another win to the equation: the fact she would be saving taxpayer dollars for prosecuting the man. She smiled knowing she would get time off by IA until they investigated, and at that time, she would take her dead partner's advice and resign from the force. Being around her baby's father had opened some areas in her brain she'd never known existed.

Li Chan was sure from the last time she and Keyshawn made love out at the Fox Point condo that he truly did have real feelings for her now. His touch was much more sensitive than a man thinking he was fucking one of his whores just for an identity check. She remembered him asking her several times about the money she was turning in when she was returning from her supposed dates, and if she was fucking and sucking off rich tricks like she'd claimed the money was coming from. When Key learned it was all from a federal fund set aside to bust all sorts of criminals, he'd laughed and fucked her a second time that day.

"Okay, Chan, I guess we don't have a choice, but if this guy shows any interest in putting a bullet in you, do what you have to and be the first shooter," Bender said.

That was the sentence she'd been waiting to hear. Li Chan knew, if her baby's father could see how she was putting it down for him, maybe he would realize not only street whores could be loyal to their men.

Li had done everything in her power to prove how much she loved Keyshawn Watson. She had provided him with information on the White brothers and there whereabouts so he could get revenge on them, and also pertinent information for him to pull off major credit card scams with the exclusive no-limit platinum cardholders. Li knew she'd surely surpassed the expectation of his new bottom-bitch Venus, who was a bad-bitch no doubt. Venus could go out and demean herself for a week, but still in that time, she could only bring home seventeen grand. That was pennies compared to some of the ways Li Chan knew how to get money.

Bender gave the order and every one got themselves in place as they prepared to break the door down for Chan. Li Chan removed her working garb, taking off the jacket and the badge that read FBI, not knowing it didn't matter. Tiahmo was way ahead of the game.

"Mrs. Watson, you and your daughter may see your husband now," the doctor said as sympathetically as he could given the circumstances. It had been a long time since anyone had referred to Tim as her husband. Keysha looked as the doctor said it; not seeing any resentment in her mother's eyes made her smile.

As the doctor showed Keysha and her mother to Tim's room, Keysha realized that Keyshawn hadn't called her back yet. She had dialed him about seven times to see if he was coming to the hospital to at least say his final goodbyes to their father. Her mother had told her she'd spoken with Keyshawn earlier and the disposition of Keyshawn's thoughts. She exclaimed she'd heard something in her son's voice; she knew his reservations were leaning toward the not-coming side.

Keysha was the only one beside Keyshawn who had Kimmie's private number and figured she would give her a call to see if she had talked to her brother. She made a mental note to do so as soon as they left the hospital. When they went inside Tim's room, he was lying propped up on several pillows watching a rerun of the old seventies sitcom *Good Times*. It was one of the episodes where Janet Jackson was playing Penny.

"I bet you never thought that girl would grow up to be a mega star," he said looking at Michele, who once was said to favor Janet in her younger days.

"I don't see why not; she is a Jackson," Michele replied, remembering some of the good old days they'd shared together, laughing and watching the same shows.

Tim could have been a good man and a great father, but he had his own vices in life which internally kept him running from place-to-place, and most of the time, female-to-female, sometimes even city-to-city, with the addiction he suffered. He hated he'd ever started using heroin because, after his first try of the poison, he'd been hooked. When he had become a junkie and got strung-out, he was sure he couldn't have that around his woman and kids.

Keyshawn was his first-born and he loved Keyshawn more than anything in the world. He and his sister were twins, but he remembered that smile on his son's face when he popped out the womb two minutes before his sister, who'd come out smiling just like her brother. It was the happiest day in his life looking at two of the most gorgeous creations he'd ever seen.

Tim somehow still felt incapable as a man. Even though he was employed, he was working at a bindery. It was work, but not at all as good as Michele's job. The fact that his subconscious played with his emotions made it virtually impossible for Tim to feel like a man. Instead of talking about it, he did what he thought would salvage his manhood. The dope that was supposed to help him, actually rid him of all the security he had left and put him on a move he would live to regret.

Since his return to Milwaukee, he'd been hearing things about his son in the streets. Everywhere he went, people told him his son was the man. Keyshawn was a pimp and he had hoes, nice cars, and the finest jewelry money could buy. Tim was even hearing his son was part owner in a nightclub. Tim was diagnosed with cancer while in Ohio in a rehab center. He knew he didn't want to come back to Milwaukee being a burden to Michele and the kids, but he also knew he couldn't leave this world without at least trying to make amends with his babies, mainly his son.

Keysha had a sad look on her face as she pulled up a seat next to her daddy. She wanted to cry, but she knew she had to be strong for Tim's sake. She thought if he saw her crying, it might make him weak and he didn't need that at all.

"So where is your brother Keyshawn these days?" Tim asked.

"That boy be busy. Ain't no telling where he is, Daddy, but I think he still may come see you from what I heard," Keysha replied, lying. She hadn't talked to him yet herself, so she was unsure if Key had any plans on coming to see their father. Keysha knew her brother was having a hard time forgiving their dad for running out on the family like he had. She'd seen just how much resentment Key had when he'd first come back from their grandmother's down in Mississippi and had seen how her and her mother were living. She knew he blamed everything on Tim.

"That would be nice of him," Tim replied, knowing Keyshawn probably wasn't going to show. Keyshawn was his blood, and before his big change-of-life events, he knew if he were Keyshawn, he wouldn't have gone to see his old man either.

"So, baby, how is this boyfriend thing going?" Tim asked.

Michele batted her eyes remembering when Keysha was just a baby how Tim use to hold her and say he was protecting her from boys. She was just getting use to her boyfriend Brandon herself and he'd ended up in jail.

"Everything is going good, Daddy. He's on vacation right now, but we're going strong as ever," Keysha said.

Her father shot her a look, but didn't want to start trying to parent too much. Tim knew what vacation meant for young men, and felt it wasn't his place to pry too far in his daughter's personal affairs. He really didn't feel he had the authority to do so. He felt it was a blessing her mother had done such a good job with her.

"So what are these doctors saying, with their so-called professional asses?" Michele asked, changing the subject.

"You know how it goes, baby, with doctors and hospitals," Tim replied, shaking his head. "They're going to keep me alive as long as the VA keeps funding these doctor bills." He smiled.

"You know no matter what happened in the past, Tim, I'm going to be right here for you," Michele said, causing Keysha to look up at her. Keysha had spent almost every day of her life with her mother and knew her as well as anybody. She'd inherited her women's intuition from her grandmother in McComb, and right now that intuition let her know her mother had never stopped loving her father.

Michele's words really touched Tim's heart when she spoke them. It meant everything to hear her say that, but still, deep down, nothing would have touched him more than to spend his last few days talking to his son. Tim knew he only had a few days left. He knew what the specialist had said, but didn't want to worry Michele or his daughter. What was happening to him was out of anyone's control.

His son Keyshawn was a Leo just like him, born one day after his date of birth, and even though Tim didn't really believe in zodiac signs, he believed his son had the same stubborn traits as he once had. Leos were said to have strong personalities and hardheads. One thing he wanted to share with his son was to tell him he was saved now; he had found God. Tim wanted to share some of the newfound-glory being saved had given him.

Michele saw the black book with the gold letters inscribed Holy Bible lying next to Tim's bed. She wondered about it, but didn't say anything to Tim. She noticed a certain amount of peace in her ex-husband's eyes. She hoped in her heart he had accepted Jesus Christ as his personal Savior so he would be in heaven when she got there. If he had, Michele knew, when Tim left this place, he would be in a much better place.

Chapter 3 ~ Man Down

The Grand Jury was finally ready to start the proceedings. The purpose of a Grand Jury hearing is to hear both sides of the story and figure out if the government had enough evidence to proceed with the case against Keyshawn Watson and T.A. Smith. They were going to have separate proceedings since the only real link the State could actually tie them to was the nightclub they shared ownership in. The prosecutor thought it would be better to tie that in later when they went after the dirty politician who had elected to help them out.

The prosecutor's real hope was maybe he could actually get one of them to testify against the other for a lesser sentence. He knew with all the charges he'd filed, even if and when they tossed a few out, both men would most likely still parole to a nursing home if he got what he wanted in the end.

Smith's proceedings were first, and it had actually been the first time Keyshawn had seen his brother since they had been detained in the federal building. The agent escorting T.A. had walked him right past Keyshawn's holding cell. As soon as they made eye contact, they threw up the deuces as T.A. passed. T.A. smiled at his boy knowing Keyshawn had turned out to be the best pimp he'd ever known. If push came to shove, his bro would at least make history for flipping a federal agent to the dark side, getting her pregnant, and knocking her for some of the State's criminal fund.

"Keep your head up," Keyshawn yelled through the solid-steel door that separated the two.

T.A. winked and headed down the corridor to meet with his attorney. T.A. and his lawyer sat in small room getting a chance to talk before T.A. had to face his accusers. The attorney had filled him in on everything going on and told him it wasn't as bad as it seemed.

"What-the-fuck does 'as bad as it seems' mean?" T.A. asked, knowing once most lawyers got their money, it was a good chance they were looking to sell you out.

"Well, Mr. Smith, they still couldn't flip your two girlfriends to testify. I tell you, those two are some tough little women."

T.A. really didn't like what he was insinuating. He knew it didn't matter what side the white man was on or how much you paid him to represent you, they all thought black people where uneducated fools who did anything to survive.

"The most damaging thing they have on you is the one girl, who admits she was enslaved by you. My argument is her claims of this crime was years before the whole investigation even started."

"So what does that mean?" T.A. asked, getting frustrated with his lawyer. "Look here, man, I'm paying you some damn-good money to represent me. Your ass has already got ten thousand, and that was just an upfront retainer, so you say. The least you can do is spare me this kindergarten-bullshit defense and keep it one hundred with a real motherfucker, no what I'm saying," he said ominously, staring at his lawyer with ice in his eyes.

"I got someone on the staff searching through some back-case law now. I need to see if I can find any loopholes in the law that will make this new witness' testimony inadmissible. It almost seems like what they're trying to pull should fall under some type of entrapment. Bringing forth a material witness who is indicating themselves in illegal activity before the activity was deemed chargeable doesn't seem right. I assure you, Mr. Smith, my people are on it."

"How in the fuck in that entrapment my man?" T.A. asked.

"You aren't going in front of the Grand Jury for anything that has to do with this witness. It's just a ploy the prosecutor is trying to use to show how long you've allegedly been engaging in human trafficking. At the same time, it should be inadmissible in court because it's your word against hers. Who's to say you even know this woman." The lawyer spoke with more confidence in his tone now.

T.A. was definitely street-smart. He had talked to a lot of the homies who had done time, and a lot of them got jailhouse law degrees, becoming penitentiary lawyers. Some of them had even filed their own paperwork, getting their cases heard on appeal. Some of them had even gone all the way up the chain of command, landing a day in Supreme Court. T.A. even had a few of the homies who had gotten time reductions and a couple had even walked, free men. But he wasn't trying to do any of that. He paid top dollar and had given money in advance in case of emergencies. Both he and Keyshawn had a little stash put aside with Big Daddy for something like this. Big Daddy had their back as well if they needed more.

"Look, man, I need you to go in here and make it do what it do. I'm not worried about a little time, see? I just don't want to spend my entire life in no fucking jail cell," T.A. said, willing to spend all his money on his freedom.

"I will give it my all, Mr. Smith; you have my word," his lawyer replied.

T.A. watched his attorney walk out the room and get prepared to defend him. He wasn't the least bit scared of the outcome. It had been so many years since he'd seen Natty. He wondered—even though she was snitching on him—how she looked now. He had hated that her jealousy had taken her down the wrong path and led her back to the streets looking for a hit of dope. But for pimp, a jealous hoe was a no-no, and he couldn't have it. Natty was supposed to be a vet bitch. He'd knocked her in an after hours joint from a well-known pimp he once looked up to. It was one of the first challenges he had encountered in the game, and he'd handled himself like a real boss. The old school pimp had shaken his hand and congratulated him on getting his bottom-bitch to choose up. He smiled reminiscing on his first trip to Las Vegas. Natty had made him forty thousand in one weekend during a Tyson fight at the MGM. That was the same night he'd realized he would spend the rest of his life macking on a hoe.

He did a little thinking for a second about his own life. He was on top of his game when the Feds finally came. He had all the finest things money could buy—the cars, the lavish trinkets, and a few pieces of prime real estate. On the streets, he had the power. He controlled some of the baddest bitches' minds the sidewalks and hotel rooms had ever seen. T.A. felt like he'd gotten everything he'd signed up for in the first place when he'd decided to pimp or die.

A part of him was glad his other homie Red wasn't there for what was going on. He looked up at the ceiling and said aloud, throwing up another peace sign, "Don't worry, my man; we got this shit here, homie."

Li Chan made it inside. When she turned to look back, she insisted the rest of the agents wait on the outside of the front door. She claimed she didn't want to ruffle the perp's feathers and have him get trigger happy.

Bender agreed to give her the opportunity, figuring this was the only chance to bring Tiahmo into federal custody safely. SAIC Bender watched as agent Li Cham walked in with her Glock drawn. As he peered on from the distance, he was hoping her two-hour-a-month negotiator's crash course had stuck with her. It was part of the agency's bylaws that every agent took a two-hour course, whether that was what he or she was going for or not.

"YOU MUTHAFUCKAS COME UP THEM STAIRS AND THERE IS GOING TO BE A LOT OF DEAD FUCKING FEDERAL AGENTS IN THE NEIGHBORHOOD TODAY! I LOVED GOVERNMENT CHEESE; NOW THERE'S GONNA BE GOVERNMENT BACON FLOATING AROUND THE HOOD!" Tiahmo belted out, hearing the noise downstairs.

"Now listen, Tiahmo, no one here has to die. This is Kimmie; let me come up and talk to you face-to-face," Li said, knowing her first attempt wasn't going to work that easily.

"WHAT?! Bitch, who you think you jacking at? You the muthafuckin reason I'm in this predicament in the first place. You ain't no hoe, bitch! You the po-po!" Tiahmo said disdainfully.

Li looked toward the door entrance, making sure none of her co-workers heard the comments coming from the upper level of the home. She knew she had to get closer to him; if not, she was going to have to answer a lot of questions when this was over—a lot more than she was anticipating answering.

"Listen, it's not what you think, Tiahmo. I'm alone and I want to come up unarmed," Li tried to explain as best she could.

"You got me once, cop chick, so you think I'm green as a muthafucka, huh? You actually think I'm going to let you come up here now? Your sneaky ass has probably got a throwaway piece strapped to your ankle, or some tear gas you're gonna try to throw at me. You muthafuckas think every nigga's stupid!"

"I said it isn't like that, Tiahmo. If they were going to send in tear gas, it would have come through the windows already."

Li knew she was losing ground. She was lost on what to do or what to say to him to make him let her up. 'This is one crazy motherfucker,' she thought. She'd watched the way he handled Daley's body and knew Tiahmo didn't have a sensitive bone in his body. What he thought about killing a federal agent was probably equivalent to what Bin Laden thought about American people.

"Listen, bitch, I've got a one-hundred-round magazine in this pretty muthafucka I'm holding, and two more lying on the bed next to me. What my man Tony Montana say? You wanna go to war, I'll take you to war!" he replied.

The sad part is she knew he meant every word. His file said he'd spent five years in Jackson State Prison, doing his last four in the hole. She knew he wasn't going back without a fight. Agent Li Chan knew from the bottom of her heart that the fool upstairs meant every word he'd chorused. He would shoot his way straight to hell rather than go back to the joint.

"I don't know how you got the best of my mans and dem bitches, but you ain't that slick to get me that way. And stop calling yourself Kimmie; you ain't no hoe!" Tiahmo demanded, peeping out the curtains as he heard a chopper hovering now.

Li felt she was at a standstill, but she also knew, if Tiahmo was taken in, it was over for her and for Keyshawn. Her cell rang. Thinking it was her boss, SAIC Bender, she reached to grab it from her side. Li was shocked to see it wasn't her regular cell phone ringing but her private throwaway. She was startled at first because she had known Keyshawn wouldn't be calling her from the Federal building. That would be too risky on the traced phones.

When she looked at the call, she saw it was Keysha's number, Keyshawn's twin sister. Agent Li Chan started not to answer the call, then a lightbulb flashed in her head. She figured this could possibly be the break she needed to get face-to-face with Tiahmo.

"Hey, this is Auntie Patrice. What's up?" Li answered, using the code name.

"Auntie P, have you seen my uncle?" Keysha asked, still talking in code.

Li Chan realized Keysha had no idea the authorities had detained her brother earlier this morning. The Feds had come early to apprehend like they always did to catch people off-guard; normal people would just be rolling over.

"I did, but the last time we talked, your Uncle P was on 27th and State, headed north," Li replied.

The street and the direction were secret coding for jail. Keysha knew exactly what she was saying. They'd chosen that word track because that particular area was once the blade for most of Milwaukee's whores who were looking to solicit to a multiple-ethnic-group of clientele. It was close to the 27th street viaduct, which separated the north side from the south side of the city. It was also three minutes from the casino, making it even more official as prime trick real estate.

The area had a lower-class strip club called Rickey's, and a block away from the strip club was an expensive steak joint called the Five O'Clock Steakhouse. That was where some of the wealthiest people made reservations daily. The area also had multiple currency advantages with a sex novelty store placed in the center, so that made it good walking for a good hoe. That was until the Milwaukee Vice Squad had run all the real women from over there. Now all you could find walking that blade was a few transvestites and other creatures of the psychosexual world.

Even though Keysha had known this day would come for her brother, she wasn't fully prepared to accept it. She and Keyshawn were very close, and she loved him more than anything in the world.

"I need you right now," Li Chan said, seizing the opportunity.

She knew Key would be mad at her for involving Keysha, but right now, she had no choice if their lives were going to be saved. Agent Li Chan walked into the kitchen making sure she was out of earshot range. She didn't need anyone standing outside the entrance who had been smashed in to hear her conversation. She quickly as possible explained everything to Keysha as vividly and as detailed as she could. Time was not on their side and she had to move like the speed of light. The chopper outside meant tear gas might be the next resolution and she couldn't allow that.

"Put that damn fool on the phone," Keysha said, not wasting time. She wanted to give Tiahmo an earful.

SAIC Bender looked at his cheap Timex watch strapped on his wrist. His agent had been on the inside now for twenty-minutes and he wasn't liking it one bit. He had just got off the phone with the prosecutor who had told him the Grand Jury was meeting and Li Chan was going to be needed as soon as possible. Bender explained the situation, telling him they had one of Agent Daley's killers trapped in a single-family home on the north side, and asked the prosecutor to stall as long as he could. Bender was pleased he had agreed.

Bender had the Special Ops team scan the house again. Using the special equipment they had, it was easy to see just where both bodies were.

"Looks like she's in the back of the house, boss, maybe the kitchen or a back room. The perp is still upstairs in the same location," the agent holding the equipment said.

"Li, what are you doing in there?" Bender silently asked himself.

"Well, fellas, she has ten more minutes; then we're going in. Remember what I said: we're to take this one alive. I want the names of the other three responsible," he commanded.

Back inside the dwelling, Agent Li was back in front of the steps leading to the area where Tiahmo was held up.

"Listen, I have someone on the phone for you who needs to speak to you. It's important you take the call," Li said.

"Bitch, this ain't no Kevin Spacey movie. I ain't talking to no damn negotiator. Y'all want me bad enough? Y'all come and get me," Tiahmo replied.

"It isn't a negotiator at all. She said to tell you her name is Pooh," Li replied.

When Tiahmo heard the name, he knew Pooh was what they called Keysha and wondered what the hell she was doing on the phone at a time like this. Tiahmo had always had a liking for Keyshawn's twin sister, but it was a line he would never cross. T.A. and Keyshawn had taken really good care of his pockets, and there was no way he wanted to mess up that payday.

"I'm just going to toss the phone up to the landing then step back until you grab it," Li explained, knowing it was still a slim chance.

When he didn't respond, she tossed the phone anyway. She threw the phone up to the second-floor landing, and it tumbled in the right direction toward the bedroom Tiahmo was in. A few seconds later, Chan saw his shadow on the wall as he reached to retrieve the phone. After three minutes, her plan was seemingly working out the way she'd intended. Tiahmo instructed her to come on up. She knew he would want the whole story before putting a bullet in her, and that was what she was banking on.

~ ❖ ~

"Boss, she's moving upwards toward the perp," the agent said.

"Okay, Li, it's show time, baby. Let's see what you got," Bender said aloud.

He hadn't been thinking at all about that Madison promotion before today, but the field was getting hectic, and losing Daley had made him think about his own family. He couldn't stand to get killed, especially not since his wife was expecting their third child.

~ ~

Upstairs, Li Chan was finally face-to-face with the man she had just been with hours ago as Kimmie. Tiahmo had sweat pouring profusely off his forehead and nose. The top of his shirt was soaking wet and the entire room reeked of loud marijuana.

"You're one crazy bitch, Kimmie. You expect me to believe you really work for Key and you here with all these damn Feds?" he asked.

"I know, I know, Tiahmo. This shit seems so far-fetched at times, I can't believe what I've gotten myself into," Li said, thinking about her next words very carefully. She knew Tiahmo was very streetwise and always ready to murder. She had to come down to his level of communication and at the same time not insult his hood-intelligence.

"I'm in love with your boy Key. Yes, I was supposed to take him down when I was undercover. That was the job, Tiahmo, but I fell in love with him!" Li exclaimed, sounding as sincere as possible.

"Bullshit, bitch! You're trained to do that shit. I should have known when I looked into them little slanted eyes you weren't no real hoe," Tiahmo said, hitting the loud blunt.

"Seriously, Tiahmo, you got to peep game here," Li said, getting to use the street lingo she'd picked up on. "How-in-the-fuck do you think you and your crew got to the White brothers so easily? Yeah, I provided that information, and let's get real, baby boy, you knew that motherfucker in the park today was a Fed because you were briefed by my dude and Tee on the deal. But what you didn't know was he was my partner, Tiahmo. He was double-crossing me when he found out I was, let me see, as he called it, straddling the fence, but I wasn't straddling at all. I'm in love with Keyshawn. Do you think if I wasn't who Keyshawn said I was, I would have allowed you to commit the murder of a federal agent? I stand to get the chair myself if this comes out."

Tiahmo laughed hysterically at what he was hearing. Agent Li didn't know why he was laughing and figured she would do one last thing. She removed her bulletproof vest and raised her shirt up, exposing the bulge growing in her stomach.

"Please blow that smoke somewhere else. I don't think Key would approve of you polluting his son lungs," she said, showing she was indeed pregnant.

"Get the fuck outta here! I'll be a monkey's uncle," Tiahmo said, looking at the proof of life in front of him.

"Damn, bitch, you got yourself in deep! I guess the pimping is really real. So, if all this is all that, what's next, bitch? 'Cause I'm not going to jail," Tiahmo replied, honoring her request and thumbing out the blunt.

"Well, yes, Tiahmo, you are going to jail, but if you keep your mouth closed, the only time you will be doing is your revocation time. They can't pin the murder on you from the testimony of two kids who were a hundred feet away in the dark. The most incriminating evidence they have is the van, which agents have already been through and didn't find any blood or traces that

Daley's body had been inside," she said, lying. She knew her teammates had found three specks of blood matching Daley's blood almost an hour ago.

Tiahmo had taken the van to a hand car wash, so he figured it was possible she was telling him the truth.

"You know I got mad love for my niggas and I respect their pimping, bitch, so I'm going to take your word on this one here, Ms. Kimmie," Tiahmo said laughing, feeling a little better now.

He was thinking everything she said had to be real. How could she not be dirty when she was there when the kill-shot was delivered to a federal agent? Besides, if she was on some bullshit, he would offer her up to her own people. That information alone would set him free. He wasn't a dummy by far and that would be his trump card if she was bullshitting him around. He smiled, thinking, *'If the bitch isn't on the side of the streets, she will become my ace in the hole.'*

"So what we gotta do?" he asked.

"Put down that heater. I'm going to cuff you and walk you out of here just like on television."

"Damn, I never thought I would be surrendering to a bitch. Fuck it! Let's do this so I can be back out here as soon as possible," Tiahmo said, finally trusting her. Tiahmo dropped his weapon and turned around so Agent Li could cuff him.

She acted as quickly as possible, removing the Glock from her back waistband.

"Come on, Kimmie, before I change my mind and kill every muthafucka out there, including you," he said.

"I don't think we have to worry about that one, partner," she replied.

Tiahmo sensed something in her tone, and when he turned back to face her, she delivered the first shot to his chest, doubling him over. The first bullet had already killed Tiahmo, but Li Chan walked up to him and shot him twice in the leg. Bending down, she picked up his semi-automatic weapon using his dead fingers, firing rounds at the entrance of the bedroom door. Li made it look like he'd taken shots at her and left her no choice but to return fire.

Agent Li Chan picked up her two-way and yelled, "SUSPECT'S DOWN! HE'S BEEN HIT! NEED BACKUP!"

Her whole team rushed the house with caution. When they found her, she was standing next to Tiahmo's dead body, her gun still smoking and drawn down on the corpse.

Bender was the last one inside. He looked at Li Chan, and all he said to her was, "I'm going to need your full report by morning."

Chapter 4 ~ A Sucka Will Always Be Exposed

There isn't a game you can play that doesn't have a winner and a loser, and that includes the game of life. If you land ten toes down, you're always winning because you have a chance to make your next move your very best move. Ten toes up and the reality of that is game over, baby. You ain't got no more muthafuckin moves left. In the streets, this move is known as 'ass out'.

This was something T.A. had told Keyshawn and Red when they sat around and chopped it up over intense chess matches against him. Keyshawn loved the way T.A. would drop knowledge on them and keep them on top of their game as he beat them consistently, checkmating them time and time again. T.A. became the best by staying numerous moves ahead of them. It was the only time during their long-term friendship he'd considered them as opponents. The method he was displaying was teaching them a lesson that would prove to be valuable in the pimp game: if a nigga didn't stay ahead of his P, he stood a great chance at losing everything he'd worked for. If one didn't believe one night could change their life, pimping wasn't for them because, in reality, one night could change a pimp's life forever.

Being a pimp, you gained a reputation as being an innovative risk taker. There was a lot more to it than most people thought, or gave the playa credit for. It wasn't just about making some woman sell her body and bring you home the money. A married man could most likely talk his wife into that if they needed bill money bad enough. That's why the pimping game consisted of real players and the real suckas who attempted to indulge in the lifestyle as well.

Keyshawn thought about Smoove for a brief second. Smoove had built a solid reputation for being one of the downest players in the game during his long tenure as a pimp. He was known as one of the most dedicated risk takers when it came to checking his paper and taking his show out on the road. But in the midst of taking a severe loss that would push his pimping to the test, he eagerly pushed what the real niggas called a representative straight to the side. He got caught slipping and let his true colors show. That slick, down-ass nigga the world thought Smoove was vanished, dissipated, floated into thin air like he worked for David Copperfield. When he couldn't accept the rules of the very game he played, he went a step too far, causing his demise and also helping to cause the launch of an investigation of some real pimps.

Pimping a bitch is about finesse and that's a big part of the game the suckas who indulge in the business missed. We all succumb to the pimp game in one way or another. McDonald's restaurants are pimps, Nike shoes pimp hard, even the energy companies are pimps—they finesse the fact we need lights to see, so they send us a bill and we check in our paper. No one in the world can get around being pimped, or manipulated as the law might call it. Either way, pimping, baby, is the American way. This was one of the spiels T.A. use to give right before he checkmated Keyshawn. He started when he saw it coming four moves out, always causing Key to try to counteract, but by time T.A. finished his last sentence, Key had to knock his king over.

The door to Keyshawn's holding cell opened and his lawyer was standing there with a federal agent ready to escort him to his hearing. It was the moment of truth for Keyshawn Watson and he would now see what fate the cards had dealt him. For the last couple of years in the streets, he had been winning. He'd stayed ten toes down with a royal flush. Now the moment had come to see if these people were going to call his bluff and lock him up, throwing away the key.

As they walked, it seemed like it was taking forever to get to the room where the proceedings were being held. If he didn't know better, he would have thought the agent had taken them on the scenic route. When they finally entered the room, the Grand Jury was waiting impatiently after being held up by the prosecutor.

Keyshawn did a visual to see if he was really up against his peers, remembering what Big Daddy had said. "They're all going to be some muthafuckas from the suburbs, young dawg, who probably can't control their own daughters." That comment echoed in his head as Key noticed the ten white people and two black people, all looking tired and frustrated like they wanted to be in the comfort of their homes tending to their own loved ones. Keyshawn didn't like the vibe he was getting from the aura in the atmosphere, but there was nothing he could do about it.

He took a seat next to his attorney, who quickly bent down and whispered something to him. Keyshawn didn't show any emotion as his attorney told him the situation that was on television earlier didn't work out so good for the bad guy. Key wanted to smile knowing Li Chan was definitely worth her weight in gold. He had street love for Tiahmo, but that was the extent of their relationship. He wasn't sure if any man could hold his tongue facing the death penalty. The only two people he trusted his life to were Red and T.A., and only one of them was still around.

The judge read over the indictment before saying anything. He was taking his time so he knew exactly what was going on. If there were two types of criminal Judge McCormick was tough on, it was drug dealers and pimps. Having lost his only daughter to the underworld, he was known to not give bail to people who committed these types of offenses, and if he was your actual trial judge, you were fucked if you were found guilty. You could almost bank on being given the maximum penalty the federal statue allowed him to give.

Although he was strict, he was also about the law. He was one who made sure the Federal Government ducks were lined up so criminals couldn't get their convictions overturned on technicalities. By day, McCormick had dedicated his life to doing away with people like Keyshawn Watson and T.A. Smith. That was a promise he'd made to his daughter when he visited her grave once a month. At night, he was just like many men in his position. He roamed the streets in his Toyota Camry, looking to buy himself some pussy, and most of those same nights, after getting laid by a whore, the evening ended with him finding solace in a bottle of expensive cognac.

Keyshawn looked at his attorney—a poker-faced man in his early fifties with a quick, bland smile. His cordial features displayed he was strictly about his paper. He sat next to Key in his two-thousand-dollar Armani suit, ready to do exactly what he was paid to do.

The session began with the prosecutor giving intricate details about the evidence they had on Keyshawn Watson, telling the Grand Jury first about the murder that happened in New Orleans, then about the murder of another pimp that was the result of the first murder out of state. The prosecutor knew the dead bodies were essential pieces in getting what he wanted. A person could be a pimp and have women selling their bodies, but over-age people made their own decisions. Of course, the offense for him was these women had been manipulated. They'd been essentially tricked by a man into thinking he loved them, and in order to keep that love everlasting, selling their bodies was what they had to do. At the end of the day, he knew like everyone else, the most secure pimps sent their women out alone and a person had free will whether to return or not.

After the prosecutor gave all his damaging evidence, it was Keyshawn's attorney's turn to go. He spoke about the case in New Orleans entering into evidence the statement from the New

Orleans detective who was handling Quesha's murder investigation. It showed Keyshawn had been cooperative with the police and he'd also gone to ID the body of the deceased. The most crucial part that worked in Keyshawn's favor was when the New Orleans detective asked what his relationship was to the deceased and Keyshawn responded Quesha was his girlfriend.

"Your Honor, I have handled numerous cases of this magnitude, and it seems like we both know there isn't a person in the world accused of what my client is accused of who would have cooperated with authorities that way. It looks to me like Mr. Watson showed genuine concern for this person."

The prosecutor shot Keyshawn's lawyer a dirty look.

"Now of course the Federal Government is only trying to do their job, but they would have you to think because a murder took place in a whole different city many moons later, they are related and my client may have knowledge or be responsible in some way. Since the Government has no evidence that shows the two deceased people even knew each other, the evidence in this matter isn't even to be considered circumstantial, Your Honor. It's all purely coincidental," he continued, bashing the prosecutor over the head.

The judge looked over the reports from the New Orleans detective. He knew Keyshawn's lawyer had made very valid points. He was hoping The People had more to go on than what they had presented, especially when they were talking about a charge that could get the defendant life. The judge handed Exhibit A, the official police report from New Orleans, to the Grand Jurors so they could review it as well. As the case went on, the prosecutor was slow-playing the time table, knowing Agent Li Chan was on her way back. He hoped the insight she would provide would be the nail in the coffin.

"It says here in the Discovery you have secured wire taps that have evidence of illegal activities going on from state to state, which also implicate this defendant in human trafficking," the judge said, tired of the waiting game himself now.

"Yes, Your Honor, we do have that—or we did. Somehow there has been a glitch in the FBI's computer database. I mean something's going on with the servers out of Berkley. I assure you they're working on them now," the prosecutor responded, knowing he was grasping for straws.

Keyshawn smiled inside because he knew the real deal. No matter how many technicians they summoned, they were never going to get those wire taps.

"I'm not really liking this one bit," the judge replied, looking over his glasses at the prosecutor.

He knew the prosecution was treading on really thin ice on this one. He'd been around twenty-one years, and he could see the bullshit coming a mile away from either side of a courtroom. Just then Li Chan walked in followed by SAIC Bender. The prosecutor finally had something to smile about.

"Your Honor, may I request a five-minute recess?" the prosecutor asked.

"A recess?" the judge chided.

"Yes. These field agents are here to testify, and they're just getting in from a hostile situation in the field. Five minutes should be all I need to brief them both," the prosecutor explained.

Keyshawn's attorney couldn't object because Li Chan's name was on the list of witnesses against him.

"Exactly five minutes, no more. One minute over and you're not going to like me. Mr. Woods," the judge said, giving a contemptuous stare at the Government's obviously-incapable mouthpiece.

Keyshawn sat with a crocodile-wide smile, wondering what Kimmie was up to. He figured once this was all over, he would legally change her first name to Kimmie since it had grown on him. He wasn't going to run around calling his bitch Li Chan. That was her police name and he really didn't like that name. He didn't want to look at her and be thinking about her federal agent name every time they spoke to one another.

Li Chan stood outside in the hallway talking with Prosecutor Woods. It wasn't the first time Woods had tried a case Chan had to testify on. He, too, was one who'd always had a secret crush on Agent Li Chan. Woods had followed her career and become infatuated, admiring Li for her courage and beauty at such a young, tender age. He looked at her as she spoke, with her mass of tangled jet-black curls and smooth vanilla toned skin. Her lips were tight, but had a sensual effect to them as if they were full. It seemed like she had put on a few pounds in the midsection and her breasts had gotten a little larger since he'd seen her last, but she was still a drop-dead gorgeous piece of flesh.

"It's really show time now, Agent Chan. Are you ready?" Woods asked, addressing her professionally.

Something didn't seem quite right to Woods. He looked at her then back at Bender. Just as Agent Chan was about to say she was ready, everything she had eaten came up. Woods just escaped being drenched in remnants of what looked like Chicken Alfredo and garlic bread. His favorite pair of David Eden's weren't so lucky though as a splash of the stinky mass landed on the tips of his shoes. Bender reached for his agent, but it was too late. Li Chan had collapsed; she'd fainted right there in the courtroom hallway. Bender was lucky he caught her before she hit the floor. He summoned one of the court officials standing around to get an ambulance.

Agent Chan knew her diversion was flawless. She wasn't at all in a comatose state. She was actually listening to everything they were saying, preparing to open her eyes by time the medics arrived. She risked some things for fear of going to any hospital. She couldn't risk anyone finding out yet she was pregnant. She just needed to make sure the medics took about twenty minutes arriving. She knew by then the jury would have been dismissed.

SAIC Bender sat at his desk on a phone call with the chief commander. After all his great work today out in the field taking down one of Daley's killers, the higher-ups still didn't respect him for the incompetence he'd showed securing the evidence in the Watson-Smith case. He sat there like a retard, constantly repeating, "Yes, sir. No, sir. I understand, sir." He said sir so many times it actually to him back to his boot-camp days when he was in Fort Dixon, training as a Green Beret. One thing about the Federal Bureau of Investigation that Bender knew oh-so-well was news traveled fast.

The fact that one of Bender's own was on leave of duty because his user name and password were responsible for deactivating the wiretaps was enough for Madison to send IA in. When those clowns came, they didn't stop until they investigated the whole department. Now Daley's killer was dead and they wouldn't have a trial in that matter as well. The others involved would remain at large, which meant three more vicious killers were still at large and capable of doing more harm.

Bender was the first to admit it took guts to murder a federal agent, especially when an off-duty federal officer had just been robbed and murdered at a gas station on Villard a year ago. The

Bureau had showed the public how seriously they took crimes like that when they'd stopped at nothing to bring in the suspect who'd done the shooting. To top it off and add to Bender's fuck-ups, Keyshawn Watson was most-likely going to make bail. That was apparent since the only charges that could be filed against him was conspiracy to commit credit card fraud and conspiracy to bribe a public official, which Bender was sure his co-defendant would eat that one all alone.

With Agent Li Chan getting sick, the State's case against Keyshawn Watson on the human trafficking was very weak. A first-rate public defender could have beaten the charges without the hardcore evidence of the wiretaps. It was amazing none of Watson's girls wanted to testify. Not even with the offer of witness protection and a new identity. They just weren't willing to cooperate at all with the Government in prosecuting Watson or Smith.

Bender leaned back in his chair behind his cluttered desk, chewing on the end of a ballpoint pen. As he looked over Agent Seth Bennis's file for the umpteenth time, he couldn't concentrate on anything but the ass-chewing he'd just taken. He also kept wondering what Keyshawn Watson have that was so special that neither one of these girls, who had never done hard time, would say anything to incriminate him.

Bender was dumbfounded by it. As many times as he'd worked one of these cases over his tenure, he had to admit he'd personally never seen anything like it. Usually when the women involved were given a chance to be free from being charged, and at the same time regain their own individualism back, they usually cracked under the smallest interrogation and gave up the goods on the pimp who'd manipulated them to have sex with other men. But for some damn reason, Keyshawn Watson had done the impossible. It was going to eat Bender alive if he didn't find out exactly what made Watson trafficker of the decade.

His phone rang again, startling him. He closed Agent Bennis's file, making a mental note in his mind that the agent had a perfect jacket.

Agent Bennis had been with the Bureau over eight years, doing all the tedious jobs without ever a complaint to be promoted. It was strange for him to go so far when he had never had any infractions documented. To his credit, Agent Bennis had never even missed a day of work, or for that matter, even been late. "Hell, the man had even declined his seven-year sabbatical," he said, knowing it didn't make sense for a person of his stature to commit a crime, hindering an investigation.

He made one more mental note before speaking to the caller to check out the agent's financials for any recent large transactions, but he was almost one hundred percent sure he wouldn't find anything in Agent Bennis's accounts.

"Bender here."

"Hey, boss, this is Agent Love. I'm out at Mendota and I think you need to make your way on out here. This Watson character is one crafty dude!" Love exclaimed.

"Damn it! We just can't get a fucking break," Bender said, listening to Agent Love. "Gimme an hour or so. I'm going to stop at the County Hospital and check on Agent Chan. She wasn't feeling well after that big standoff. So yeah, I say maybe an hour, hour-and-a-half; I'll be there," Bender continued, checking his Timex again.

"Okay, boss; I'll grab a bite in the cafeteria and wait on you," Love replied.

"Hey, Love," Bender said before hanging up.

"Yeah, boss. Is there something else you need me to check on?"

"Yeah: be careful eating the food at that crazy home." he said.

"What's that, boss?"

"I heard from a reliable source they put all sorts of shit in their food to keep people the patients under control," Bender laughed before hanging up.

Chapter 5 ~ The House on the Hill

Keysha Watson pulled the black Lexus GS 300 in the parking lot in Franklin, Wisconsin. She had promised Brandon she wouldn't miss any visiting day as long as he was there, and she had stuck to her promise thus far. When she said those words, Brandon had made sure she would never have to catch the charter bus to come see him like most inmates' girlfriends had to do. The day he was sentenced, he left her the new luxury sedan he'd bought while he was out on bail.

Brandon loved and trusted Keysha so much he'd also given her the debit card to his bank account, which had enough money in it to cover what ever purchases she needed to make. He wanted to make sure she never had to worry about anything besides school. Keysha was dependable and had never spent over her daily limit, and she kept fifty dollars a week on his books so he could order noodles and goodies to get him through the long, lonely nights without her.

At the House of Corrections, the visitors were no longer searched at the front entrance when visiting inmates. The State had changed the system to a non-contact visiting facility. You still had to go through a metal detector, but now when you came to visit a loved one, all you got to do was sit behind a five-inch-thick glass window with wire running through it and talk on a stinky phone while looking at each other. Keysha hated the fact she couldn't touch or kiss the man she was in love with and hoping one day to marry.

Keysha was told by a short, stubborn-looking woman wearing a stained, brown correctional uniform to wait in booth eleven. The mean-looking woman told her Brandon was being summoned from his unit. Keysha sat looking at all the other females there to visit their men. The House was multi-purpose. Some of the men were sentenced to do their short time there, and some of them were waiting court dates to see if they were going to the big house. She was so glad they hadn't sent Brandon up north to a State prison.

On her last visit, one girl was complaining they'd given her dude five years there and how much bullshit that was. Keysha didn't understand until she kept talking to another girl next to her with a long sew-in ponytail that looked like it needed help. That girl said it was her guy's second time there so she knew the ropes well. She explained the good time there was a bunch of bullshit, and if they had sent her baby-daddy to prison, he would have been in a half-way program in most likely two years with the five year bid he'd received. Another girl who was listening cracked her gum loudly and agreed it was bullshit.

They continued talking and Keysha was tripping when she heard the other girl explain her man was there for domestic violence. She kept saying she hadn't even pressed charges because he loved her and they were getting married while he was in there.

Another tacky-looking girl had her baby with her who wouldn't stop crying the whole time and she wouldn't stop cursing the newborn-child out. It was obvious the baby was either hungry or had soaked its diaper. Keysha looked and didn't see the young girl, who looked to be barely eighteen, even had a diaper bag with her. It made her think about all her problems with school and how hard college was. Keysha realized at that moment she wasn't really that bad off at all, not compared to other women in the world her age.

Her visits to Brandon usually came later on in the evening when it was the last go round. Keysha did that purposely so Brandon would think of her when it was time to go to bed at night. Today she had come earlier, only because she wanted to tell him what was going on with her brother Keyshawn. She had yet to talk to her mother to let her know Keyshawn was locked up, feeling it would be a bit much given her father's condition.

That's why she'd decided to come see her man. Brandon was smart and he'd always given her sound advice that she'd cherished. That was something she admired a lot about Brandon—not only was he a beast in bed, he was street-smart mixed with book-smarts and knew something about almost everything. Her professor at school told her she was what was called a sapiosexual when he heard her talk about Brandon so much. She had no idea what the word meant, but when she looked it up, her teacher was right on point.

Booth twelve was next to her on her right, and there was a heavyset white girl sitting there, breathing hard. She was carrying the cutest little baby boy with the curliest sandy-brown hair Keysha had ever seen. The baby was quiet and smiling like he was very happy with life. His clothes were clean and the toy in his hand was new. Keysha knew his mother must take good care of him.

The baby's father came down to the visiting room before Brandon. He did a double-take when he saw Keysha's pretty face. She couldn't believe he'd stopped and eyed her the way he had. It was a very disrespectful gesture toward his girl, who didn't say a word. Keysha started to say something, but she let it ride because the white girl probably had no business messing with a nigga like him anyway. She looked like the type from the suburbs whose parents had probably disowned her by now for her choices in men.

Brandon was two minutes behind the dude with the white girl in the next booth. Brandon loved it when Keysha came to see him. He was smiling ear-to-ear when he sat down, looking in the dark-brown eyes of his future wife. The neck of his shirt was a little wet with sweat, and Keysha figured he must have come from the gym playing basketball.

Everyone in there wanted Brandon on their team when they got a chance to go to the gym. Since he'd played two-guard in college at UWM and was known for scoring, he was almost like an idol to the other guys in there with him. When he first got there, he'd tried to conceal his identity. It was almost impossible since his case was front-page news and all criminals did was read the paper and hood books. The media had followed Brandon's case like he was Pablo Escobar or some major cartel player moving semi-trucks full of weed.

"Hey sexy mama," he said, looking at his woman. "When did you do that to your hair?" Brandon asked, checking out Keysha's new hairdo. One thing about Brandon, he didn't care how much of his savings she spent. He knew she wouldn't go overboard.

"What? You don't like it or something, bae?" she asked, making a sad face before he answered.

"Come on now, girl. I love it. You know I hate it with a passion when women put all that extra hair that ain't theirs in their head," he said, smiling. Brandon was glad Keysha never wore weave or braids or even fake nails. She had cut her own hair in a nice low style that fitted her face perfectly.

"You changed your visiting time, I see. What if my other girl was here seeing me?" Brandon playfully said.

He was joking because last time Keysha was there, this had actually happened to a dude. The guards had let two chicks in at the same time, and the two women were fighting like cats and dogs. They had both ended up getting charged and both of dude's kids had gotten picked up by Child Protective Services.

"Well, if she was, we would have had to decide who was going to sit on whose lap, and split the time up," Keysha replied, telling a joke of her own.

"Damn, I feel like big bro Key now," he said, laughing hard.

"Keep it up and get that ass kicked when you get out." She laughed herself. "But seriously, bae, that's what I came to talk to you about, my brother Keyshawn," Keysha said, getting his full attention now.

"Is bro okay? He ain't get fucked up, did he?" Brandon asked with sure concern for the dude he looked up to.

"Keyshawn has been federally indicted. You didn't see the news today?" she asked.

"Yeah, I saw something. I mean, bro wasn't on there but I saw some fool had a standoff with the Feds and got himself killed—crazy muthafucka, thinking he could shoot it out with them people. Wait . . . that wasn't . . .?"

"No, silly, but that was one of his dudes," she replied.

Keysha spent the whole thirty minutes allowed for visitation filling Brandon in on some stuff he didn't know about. All Brandon could do was praise his future brother-in-law even more when he heard the details. Brandon had known he wanted to be under the tutelage of Key when he first met him. He had been getting some bogus numbers on product from his old supplier, which wasn't leaving him much room to profit. Then, out of nowhere, comes this dude giving him some sweet plays on the weed, allowing him to really see some daylight. Messing with Keyshawn, Brandon had stashed over $150,000 in no time. That was one of the major reasons he didn't mind the little time he'd gotten for his case.

"Wrap it up," a guard called out.

Brandon and Keysha knew that meant all visitors had about sixty seconds to say their goodbyes. The new captain who ran the place had strict rules; if you didn't wrap up your visit and get in line to head back to your dormitory, they would cancel your visits for ninety days.

"Okay, baby, I'm going to take your advice and tell mama when I get home," Keysha said, standing up and giving Brandon a nice eyeshot of her camel-toe print through her jeans. He hadn't been gone that long, but he missed the feel of her thick hips underneath him.

"Cool; I will call you in the morning to check on you," he replied, getting instantly hard looking at her pussy and the pretty face of the only woman he'd ever truly loved. Keysha blew a kiss as he went to line up with the other inmates. She looked at her watch and saw they'd finished with ten seconds to spare.

In line, all the inmates chatted and bragged on who had the finest bitch on the visit, who had the ugliest, and whose girl was going to bless their books with some funds to order commissary. The dude who was in the next booth with the white girl made his way close to Brandon. He complimented Brandon on how good Keysha looked and asked if she was his baby-mama.

Brandon had seen the dude around, but didn't really know him well enough to be answering personal questions. Brandon just looked at him and nodded his head. He kept trying to pry and asked Brandon what grade school Keysha had attended, claiming Keysha looked familiar to him. Brandon looked at the dude like he was crazy and kept on walking.

Chapter 6 ~ Man Not Down

Keyshawn Watson smiled as he walked from the confinements of the federal holding building back onto the streets of Milwaukee. As his checkered-suede Timberlands hit the pavement, he knew it was far from over for him. He was just glad what they had charged him with, the judge had had no choice but to grant Keyshawn a modest bail. Twenty-five bands were no problem for him to arrange to be posted. Keyshawn smiled when his lawyer looked at him and said, "Old suit isn't that bad." All he could think about was a lyric from the old school rapper Ice-T he use to admire: *The streets to a playa is the place to be.*

As bad as he wanted to, Key didn't risk calling anyone from inside the Federal building He knew every call, except attorney/client calls, was monitored and recorded from inside the jail, and if you said something you weren't supposed to, they would use it against you in the courtroom. He wasn't really quite sold on the fact the attorney/client calls weren't being monitored. It was sad for anyone who trusted the law. They were pimps, too.

When they got the amount of the bail, Keyshawn had had his lawyer contact Big Daddy to get the ends together. Just as they had always planned, Big Daddy dropped the paper off to the attorney's office, and Keyshawn was a free man. It was supposed to work the same way for his best friend as well. Keyshawn looked at the building behind him and thought about T.A. for a brief moment. He hoped like hell his homeboy caught a break.

Key flagged down a cab to Big Daddy's establishment, where he knew Big Daddy would be waiting on him. It was the first time in a long time Keyshawn had no money in his pocket and no cell phone to make calls on. The predicament felt really odd but he was okay with it. His name was power and that was one of the main things he had hustled so hard for, but he'd felt a bit financially helpless. It was the first time in a long time Keyshawn had felt helpless since his return from McComb, Mississippi, several years ago. That day was still etched in his mind, coming home to a home that wasn't suitable for a rodent to live in. He would never forget any of that.

Ten minutes later, the repainted burgundy Chevy Impala that was being used as an American Taxi pulled up in front of the club Big Daddy owned. It was funny how a company named themselves American but had all foreign drivers pushing their whips. It seemed like ever since nine-eleven the Arabs had given up cab driving and had relinquished it to the Africans and Jamaicans— knowing real Americans were some grudge holders, even against an entire race who had had nothing to do with the initial problem. They'd gone to selling nachos in corner stores because their lives were in danger behind the wheel, but with the tax credits and other breaks our so-called American Government gave them, it was easy for them to move on to bigger and better things—like owning all the neighborhood stores and gas stations.

Keyshawn's homie Bone was waiting outside for him as the rain drizzled a bit and the windshield wipers squeaked to keep the front window clear. When Key stepped out the taxi, the African man looked back with a menacing look. Speaking loudly and spitting with a heavy accent, Keyshawn knew the man was demanding his fare.

"Hold da' fuck up, partner!" Keyshawn said, furious at being spoken to like he was a sucka.

"Me no hold up nuttin'. Me want me money fo' dis here ride," the cabbie replied, still barely comprehensible.

Keyshawn couldn't help but laugh at the extra dark-skinned man when he spoke. The cab driver didn't see anything funny and wondered what the hell his passenger found so hilarious. Keyshawn was thinking about a comedian who played like he was from Africa. The guy was really an American comic, but made a living funning the people from the Motherland. His favorite line when he performed was, "Me a bish-ass mutafucka." Somehow he'd coined that shit and had some mild success landing a role in a few movies pretending.

Bone saw what was transpiring and handed the driver a fifty dollar bill. Then he mean-mugged the driver very intensely. It was away of letting him know not to get too verbally out-of-order with his friend. "You can keep that little chump change, too, black man," Bone said, hugging his boy happy to see him, forgetting all about the cabbie now.

"Man, I guess that shit is true, huh?" Keyshawn asked.

"What's that?" Bone asked.

"Them Zimbabwe muthafuckas really don't like niggas—like they ain't niggas themselves," Keyshawn laughed.

"Nigga please. Fuck that lion-choking-ass fool!" Bone replied, laughing.

The cab driver looked out the window at the two of them and just shook his head. He quickly slipped his knife back under his front seat and drove off without saying another word.

"Man, I'm glad you're home, big homie. I told your ass gambling is where it's at, my nigga. Them muthafuckin people ain't never going to be looking for me, not long as I keep betting the dice don't six-eight, homie," Bone said, fucking with Keyshawn.

"Well, you keep risking yours trying to break these already-broke-ass niggas out here. I'm going to keep these here Tims in a bitch's ass twenty-four/seven and she gonna get mine, playa, from six in da morning to eight in the evening," Keyshawn replied, getting slick with the tongue like he always did. They shared a laugh at his comeback, knowing that he was serious about it.

"No sweat, playa; more for me. I just know I couldn't be that damn patient to be fucking with one of them funky-ass hoes. See now, the way I see it, playa, every time the dice rolls, somebody's making some loot. And the way my dice and my bank account are set up, well, let's just say these fools been doing more depositing for me lately than withdrawing," Bone replied, shaking a pair of trick dice he'd had shipped in from China.

"Hey, Key, on the real, Big Daddy's inside waiting on you, big homie.
Let's get on in here so you niggas can chop it up."

"Thanks, lil homie. I'd better get on in here and holla at the fam. You know I'm surprised I ain't got grey hair behind all this punk-ass bullshit," Keyshawn replied.

In actuality, Bone was twice the size of Keyshawn and a few years older as well, but on the streets, the term lil homie and big homie went by the weight your name carried. You could be four-nine and a buck-ten soaking wet, but if your paper touched the ceiling, you were big homie to everyone around you.

Keyshawn walked inside the club Big Daddy owned, glad he had a player like Big Daddy in his corner. The place wasn't open for business yet, but there were a few of Big Daddy's closest personal friends sitting at the bar having a business conversation and sharing a bottle of 1738, that top-shelf Remy Martin that's considered a playa's drink in the hood. Big Daddy's joint was nice; it wasn't as state-of-the-art as Key and T.A.'s club, but he was clocking paper out of there like crazy.

The major thing that came into play, and he'd tried to instill in Keyshawn and T.A., was he was getting longevity money where those people didn't fuck with him. Big Daddy had paid his dues to the streets years ago. Now he paid taxes and lived like he was a normal businessman, doing righteous things. There weren't many niggas ten-toes-down who'd played the game as hard as he once had who could put that same claim to fame out there in the free world. The niggas from Big Daddy's era were either serving all day in some joint, or all day in the ground, ASS OUT. Key walked to the back where Big Daddy's office was and rapped lightly on the door.

"Come in, Neph; I'm almost done with this call."

Key took a seat in the same seat he had been in the other day when Big Daddy had dropped on him some real playa knowledge. He admired Big Daddy a lot for his short-term run in the streets. He had hustled all avenues when he was in the game—sold dope, pussy, and credit card scams—made a bank roll, opened a club, and got out. Every now and then, he still did a little loan sharking, but that was it for him, as far as he wanted to go.

The streets had gotten ugly and the new players entering the game didn't roll with any type of code of ethics. The same nigga you got money with would be the same nigga who put you in the mix, either with the jackers or with them people if the heat got on his ass. It was just too dangerous for Big Daddy. He always said his twenty-grand-a-week take-home was just fine for him.

Big Daddy finally finished up on his phone call and directed his attention to Keyshawn. "Damn, neph, you a lucky nigga; you know that, right? I mean a nigga got scooped by them white folks and you're home in less than twenty-four hours. That shit is unheard of, lil dawg!" Big Daddy exclaimed.

"I know, and really, Unc, to keep this shit P, I owe it all to a bitch. That bitch Kimmie put in the work to keep a nigga free. All this pimping I'm doing, stacking all this paper, none of it would mean shit if I was behind bars doing a bid," Key replied.

"Didn't you say you got the broad knocked up, too?" he asked.

"Yeah; lil mama's damn-near 'bout to start showing in a sec."

"Boy, let me tell you something. You got that little funny-looking bitch's heart. See, Keyshawn, it's one thing to take one of these hood bitches and turn her out. Now, when I say hood bitches doesn't mean the bitch doesn't have a degree. She could even be a smart broad, have some type of Master's in something. I'm saying a bitch who is from the trenches, may have lived this ghetto life once upon a time—them type of bitches. You know what I'm saying," Big Daddy said.

Keyshawn nodded his head, knowing exactly what he was saying.

"No matter who they are, that type of bitch can have a relapse in the blink of an eye," he continued, snapping his fingers.

"I feel you, Unc; I really do," Key replied.

"I wouldn't be surprised if you'd come and told me you'd flipped out that billionaire black bitch from the hood who has a talk show and her own network. 'Cause that bitch is off Atkinson. But a bitch who has never been exposed to nothing but the finer things in life, the ghetto where she's from is full of computer chip companies and missile builders, Neph. You just don't get to turn them broads out. You got something special inside you, Neph. You'd better believe that."

"Now let's get down to business," he said, knowing Keyshawn had to get his stable out on bail.

"Man, they're still holding my people on them punk-ass credit card charges. My lawyer said, since a couple of the purchases were high-dollar amounts, the prosecutor was going to keep it federal," Key explained.

"Listen here, baby boy, don't you know they're gonna apply as much pressure to them bitches clitorises, hoping one of them busts a nut so big her mouth cums with a story about you."

"Yeah, I kind of figured that, too."

"You're doing the right thing getting them hoes out, but what you have to do is make them hoes job up for now. Them bitches have to flip burgers, do hair, anything but sell pussy, because if anyone of them is caught while on bail, trust me, that shit's going to fall back on you. Now how much is each one of their release fee?" he asked.

Venus had the highest bail of twenty thousand; everyone else's bond was ten grand. Keyshawn knew that was because the photos they had from New Orleans showed she'd been down the longest, plus she had been identified as the one making most of the transactions with the jewelers.

"That isn't a problem. We'll arrange for that to happen in the morning. I know they're trying to fuck our boy, but T.A. is a strong nigga. I think he had his mind set for this little vacation." Big Daddy said.

"Why you say that, Unc?" Keyshawn asked.

"He came to see me the other day and said, if anything happened to him, to give you this." Big Daddy clicked open a wall safe behind his desk and removed a package. When Keyshawn opened it to see what it was, there was two hundred fifty thousand in cash and a CD.

"I don't think you'll find Marvin Gaye's greatest hits on that disc," Big Daddy said as he handed Keyshawn the package. "So I guess you'd better get going. I've got this handled for you."

"Hey, Unc, you got a Bernie Mac lying around?" Keyshawn asked.

Big Daddy opened his top drawer, removed an old, grey flip-phone, and tossed it to Keyshawn. He also threw him a set of keys to the Corsica parked out back which was used to make liquor runs at night to his cousin Shugg's liquor store in case the club ran out of anything. Keyshawn was glad Big Daddy had a burnout phone line so he could try to reach Kimmie.

"Thanks, Unc. I'll holla atcha tomorrow for sure."

Keyshawn took the package with the money and the disc, and wondered what was on the disc. The nigga T.A. had always been a surprise, and Keyshawn knew that was because he always stayed two moves ahead of the game. That was what made him the best chess player in the Midwest.

SAIC Bender cursed loudly as he walked through the underground parking structure looking for his car. He hated that the department made every unmarked unit look alike. Finally after a few minutes he found his all-black, new-body-style Dodge Avenger sitting between two more identical ones. When he got inside, he threw Agent Bennis's file on the backseat and headed out into traffic.

It had just stopped raining, and the traffic was heavy and slow-moving as he headed to the I-94 ramp that would take him to Madison West toward the County Hospital. He hoped Agent Li Chan was okay and that nothing was seriously wrong with her. He knew he wouldn't see her report until the morning now, but whatever had happened inside the residence earlier, she had done an outstanding job. It made him look good as well, and she deserved a medal for her courage and all her undercover work.

Bender almost rear-ended some elderly man driving a pickup truck who had stopped at a flashing yellow light on the freeway ramp. He blew the horn, pissed at the old man. "I don't know why this damn city lets these old people out here without checking them out," he said out loud.

Normally Bender was a great driver. He had always been a defensive driver, being in so many high-speed chases over the years, but he knew he wasn't as focused as he usually was when he was behind the wheel. Numerous things vied back and forth in his head for attention, and he couldn't pick one because each of them carried a unanimous amount of weight.

The biggest issue he had right now was Keyshawn Watson and his illegal activities. SAIC Bender had dealt with pimps who had been on the top of their game before. He had even been in charge of the case that had sent the infamous pimp to jail who'd chosen to handle Judge McCormick's daughter as a whore. The Las Vegas pimp was bought to justice and sentenced to forty years for his run in the illicit world of human trafficking.

It was crazy to Bender when he heard the stories of how he would bathe them in rubbing alcohol and make the other women watch as he set the one on fire. Once she was lit up, he would throw ice cubes on her. Or the one story that really turned Benders stomach —when his bottom-bitch was getting ready to choose up with another pimp, he'd taken a wire hanger and surgically removed five grand she concealed up inside her uterus. That was going to be the pay she gave to the new pimp to show her worth.

Bender knew these were the kinds of things pimps did on a regular basis to the women who belittled themselves for love. They were known to find the smallest thing to punish them for, making a statement to the other women that egg shells were the new Red Bottoms. You walked lightly or got the punishment you'd just witnessed your wife-in-law suffer.

Something was extremely different about Keyshawn Watson though. Bender thought he had something on the women he possessed that was totally unknown to the department. Bender thought more about the intricate details as he swerved to stay in his lane, looking over at the Milwaukee Brewers' stadium from the highway where his favorite team played baseball.

As he drove on, he started to recall the interrogations of each one of Keyshawn's girls, remembering Venus had been around the longest now, since the death of the girl in New Orleans. The tattoo on her neck showed she had a lot of respect and love for the dead girl, who was obviously her ex-coworker. Venus' attire when she was picked up was all name-brand and not the knock-off shit most pimps sent their stable out to work in either. The black knee-high Manolo Blahnik alligator-skin boots alone would cost him three months of his hard-earned salary. He knew he would get sucked off every night if he showed up home with a pair for his wife. Each one of the girls had exquisite belongings nice enough they could easily have been mistaken for a businesswoman or one of them crazy-ass basketball wives who came on television.

'It had to be more though,' Bender thought, *'unless all their self-esteems were that low who they sold their souls to the devil for a funky pair of Stuart Weitzman stilettos.'*

He banged the steering wheel, very upset with himself. No one in all his time at the Bureau had ever made him look like he took the yellow bus to work wearing a special helmet and drooling on his shirt like he was a fucking retard. Keyshawn Watson wasn't going to be the first either to succeed at pulling off the unbelievable. SAIC was the acronym for special agent in charge and that he was. Shit had to get real; it was just about to become personal to Bender now. There was no way he was going to let some black kid who didn't know his own ass from a hole in the ground outsmart him and his years of intelligence that even people like Escobar couldn't get around.

Bender had got word that bail was being arranged for each one of the girls on the case as well. He felt he had to put a man on each one of them. They were on bail, so whatever they did, they had to do it right in the city now. If the saying that the street miscreants lived by was true, once a hustler always a hustler. Keyshawn Watson would be back in business by morning.

Bender pulled into the hospital parking lot, taking a space near the door that had a sign reading, 'Police Vehicles Only'. He hated now, as he thought about Agent Li Chan, he'd pulled her out so early on the Watson case. He'd thought everything was as good as it could possibly get and she was no longer needed. Agent Chan had proven to be more than he'd expected from an undercover agent. He felt there was nothing anyone could do about her unexpected sickness, but he still felt strongly he should've let her stay until the day of the Grand Jury, then yanked her at the last minute.

SAIC Bender flashed his gold badge to the hospital security, knowing that his seventeen-shot Glock would set the metal detector off like a school bell, causing momentary confusion. The two men watching the cameras system looked up and waved him through when the saw the gold badge and ID bearing the big black letters FBI.

Bender proceeded to the front counter to ask what room his comrade was in, still oblivious to the hoax Agent Chan had pulled. He waited for a few minutes while the receptionist did some checking for him. Bender was shocked to find out Li had been discharged already. The heavyset lady in the light-blue uniform said it had been almost an hour since Agent Chan was discharged. She couldn't release any information regarding the patient's condition so Bender knew not to ask.

He wondered why she hadn't called him to check in. He tried her cell phone and it went straight to voicemail. After the second try, he left a message and decided she was probably home resting.

Bender knew as well as anyone the job could cause a person to become stressed. He dialed Agent Love to let him know he would be pulling in the parking lot shortly.

"I don't know, boss," Agent Love said, coughing.

"What's wrong?" Bender asked with concern.

"I think they gave me one of the crazy patients here's tuna sandwich by accident," Agent Love said.

"I've been throwing up blood constantly and the last time something came up I swear to living Jesus it looked like my intestines had come out," he replied, making SAIC Bender really nervous.

Agent Love could hear in his boss' voice he was very concerned about his condition and decided not to take the joke any further. But he felt it suited Bender right for always joking and fucking with all the other agents on the force.

"Just sit tight. I'm running out of here now," Bender replied.

"I'm kidding, boss; don't shit your boxers yet," Love laughed. "Just come on. I'm waiting on you. I will be posted on the first floor in the family room. They have an awesome set of *National Geographic's* here," Love said, hanging up before Bender let him have it.

Chapter 7 ~ A Day in the Life

T.A. sat in his cell thinking about his entire life before him. Even though he was still a young man, he knew the game had been real good to him. Cold but fair was another code all true players lived by. He knew he'd had a short but lucrative run in the pimp game, which had entitled him to some of the finest things money could buy. The fact he knew the system was about to lay him down for a long period of time didn't really faze him. He was more concerned with his main man, Keyshawn. When he gave Keyshawn the game, he'd felt deep down he was raising a real nigga to proceed to the throne he was sitting on, and he knew no other nigga he'd kicked it with was as capable as Key was.

The violence that came along with playing in the streets was imminent when you played the game at certain levels. Jealousy and envy were two deadly sins that consumed the suckas who were dedicated to the life of the streets. In the hearts of many lay the urge to knock a playa off his square, to make deadly attempts to relieve him of his razzmatazz and hoes, then consciously attempt to belittle a real nigga's accomplishments.

T.A. was a man of precise calculations. He made every move he'd made over the last month with extreme caution, knowing them people were coming for him and his empire. He knew the day would come for their arrival at his front door. There was no use running and hiding from the Feds; their jurisdiction spread worldwide, and where they didn't go, they would just send the marshals to cover for them. Them coming only got T.A. ready, so when it did finally become his move, T.A. was going to be prepared. He wasn't even tipping his king over for the police. If they wanted a checkmate, they would have to show they were way better than him.

The first thing was already in order as far as he was concerned. It was simply that the streets needed to know his crew was the real deal and wasn't ever going to be marked as targets for the suckas to prey upon. The violent murders that had been committed were the necessary links to survival of the game. Some things had to be done a certain way when someone got in your business in a detrimental way. T.A. was a firm believer that, if the message you were trying to convey was supposed to have a powerful impact, you'd better damn-near send a nigga's head home to his mama in a cake box. That's why he had mad love for his homeboy. His nigga Tiahmo didn't fuck around. When he sent a message, it got delivered like the mafia had been through to show you they meant business. As far as T.A. was concerned, you didn't fuck with two things: his money and his two brothers. The price to pay was serious if you did.

He stared at the ceiling in his cell, smiling, knowing Keyshawn would be okay from this point forward. He knew the Feds would pull out every trick in the book on both of them. When they came to try to implicate Keyshawn in the bribery of a public official, they had no win. It wasn't a coincidence that T.A. kept the business end of the club paperwork for him and Red, but if anything ever came down, he knew all three of them couldn't get fucked up if they didn't have any idea what happened. T.A. knew he would take the weight for that as well.

It had worked out just as he planned. The Feds always thought they were one step of everyone they detained because of their trumped-up conviction rate. But T.A. knew it was easy to be so effective when you set the stage as they did. They made sure you faced so much time that a nigga hardly ever took a Fed case to trial —that was if he ever wanted to see daylight again. Their ways of sentencing you by guidelines and enhancers made a nigga tell on his mama and beg for an offer. T.A. was no fool though. He needed his partner to stay on the streets and take care of business while he was gone. There was no use of both of them sharing a cell for thirty years in some federal joint. Most niggas didn't think that way though nowadays, but T.A. knew whatever time he had to do, his man would make sure he did it in style. There was no doubt in his mind.

T.A. crossed his legs and rested his hands behind his head, lying on the cheap, thin plastic pillow they provided for detainees. He knew he should have killed Natty way back then when all the bullshit jumped off with her. It might have been the only bad move in the game he'd ever made, but even he knew the feelings he had for Natty were real when they were together—he as her pimp and she as his bottom-bitch. Natty had been his first hoe, a real go-getter and single-handedly she was the one who had put her daddy on the map as a true pimp. She had taught him things being older that had made him the sharpest knife in the drawer.

His young mind at the time was still strong on what he wanted from the game, but he couldn't bring himself to put bricks on her ankles and sink her life as he should have. That was all a mute point now. T.A. knew every real nigga who played in the streets would make a mistake once or twice. Some mistakes you got a chance to overcome the results of and some you didn't. From a pimp's perspective, he'd known Natty was a hoe scorned. Now, after all these years, that scorned hoe was finally getting her sweet revenge on him for letting her live. It was bittersweet, but T.A. was a player, and as hard as it was to accept those facts, he understood it came with the territory. To T.A. Smith, he had to chalk it up: it was all in the day of the life.

~ ❖ ~

Keyshawn woke up ready to get the day started. He hadn't slept well because he was worried about Kimmie. She hadn't called him, which he knew wasn't possible because she didn't have a number to reach him, but he knew she had to know by now he was a free man. She did have a key to the condo and could have come by. Maybe that may have been too risky as well since her last partner had been following her and tried setting her up. Keyshawn was very familiar with the two cousins, drama and karma. They were definitely related to one another and his life had become tainted by both of them.

He rolled over looking at the alarm clock from Sharper Image Venus had ordered for him. Big Daddy had promised to handle all that, and he knew they all should be released in the next hour or so. Keyshawn had so much on his mind he hadn't even called his family to let them know he was all right, knowing his mother and sister were probably sick with worry.

He got up from his king-size bed, throwing on his slippers, walking through his home and making a visual observation of the damage. The place was still in disarray from when the Feds had come and scooped him the other morning. The agents who showed up there had torn up his walls looking for currency and anything else that may have been hidden inside them.

He did a second observation of his place, shaking his head. They had done a real number, trashing the pillows on his expensive Italian leather couches, and cutting it open and removing the cushions down to the wood in search of evidence. Keyshawn felt it was more out of jealousy than their actual protocol. Haters weren't just the niggas on the streets, but some of them came in uniforms and held high-ranking jobs such as law officials.

He walked in his kitchen and fixed himself a bowl of Captain Crunch cereal, taking a seat on one of the stools under the marble countertop. So many things flashed through his mind simultaneously that his brain couldn't rest to select even one proper thought. It was always in times like these that he could pick up the phone and either call Red or T.A. just to hear the voice of someone he knew had their shit together. Both of his confidants were gone in one way or another, so that option was no longer available for him to choose.

Keyshawn looked at the burnout phone he'd gotten from Big Daddy for a second and decided there was one other voice that could help sooth his nerves. He picked the phone up and dialed the number, almost hanging up on the first ring. When his grandmother answered, somehow she'd already known it was him before he even got the chance to say, "Hello, Grandma." There was something special about that woman's voice he had missed.

"I'm not going to go into any lectures with you, Keyshawn. All I can say is that by the grace of God you're safe."

"Thanks, Grandma. It feels good to actually feel safe," he replied.

"I will tell you this: the Lord doesn't make mistakes. Everything we do in life is predestined by His will, and here on earth, God's will will be done," she said, making him think.

Keyshawn knew exactly what type of conversation he was going to be in for when he'd dialed her. He believed in God, but he wasn't really the religious-type dude to take it as far as some people.

"How are those tired girls, baby? I'm sure they're resting themselves up 'bout now," she asked.

"They're all doing okay, Grandma."

"Why haven't you called your mama and sister yet? You know they're over there worrying about you like two crazy people. I told them to just pray for you like I did. Somehow I knew you would be all right but, baby, you know this ain't nothing but the Lord talking to you. Keyshawn, you've got a chance to change yourself and turn your life around, but you can't keep cheating death. It won't continue to lose if you keep playing around."

"I know. I've got a lot of thinking to do, Grandma. I assure you I'm going to make some changes in my life," Keyshawn said, knowing he had to make some real changes. He just wasn't sure what they were going to be. Somehow talking to his grandmother always took him back to his childhood. No matter how tough he was in the streets and on his hoes, his grandmother was that one person in his life who always knew what to say, how to say it, and when it should be said. She had impeccable timing with him.

"Now there is one other thing I want to talk to you about seriously, Keyshawn."

"I'm listening, Grandma."

"Now you know I never really liked Tim, but I've learned a lot of things growing old, and he is still one of God's children. I've been telling you this since you were knee-high and I'm going to say it again, son: we all fall short of the glory of God."

It wasn't the first time his grandmother had said that to him, and Keyshawn knew exactly why she repeated it to him at this moment. His life was marked with gaiety and he still had a lot of people who loved him dearly, despite all his faults. The people who judged him were the people who were suppose to judge him. The people who loved him loved him no matter what the people who judged him thought.

He knew he couldn't continue blaming his father for everything bad that had happened to him. When he'd come back from Mississippi, he was going to hustle regardless of whether his mother and sister lived in that rat hole they'd once lived in or on Lake Drive. It was just the truth of the matter. Blaming his father Tim was just an excuse for him to feel better about it inside. Blaming his environment was something society gave young black men as a separate excuse. He had made his mind up he was going to talk to his father to at least try to make amends. He was going to be a father now and knew he wouldn't want his child to go through life hating him because of certain things he'd done.

"Okay, Grandma, I got you," Keyshawn said before ending the call.

Keysha woke up when her toss-away phone started ringing on her nightstand. Lately she wasn't staying over to the apartment her and Brandon had recently gotten. She had been staying at her mother's place. There were only two people in the world who had that number and one of them was in jail, so she automatically assumed it was Kimmie calling with news about her brother's predicament. Not looking at the number display, she answered. Keysha jumped when she heard her brother's voice, pulling the covers over her naked body.

"Damn, Key! You all right in there?" she asked.

"I could stand a maid to get this mess up, but I'm all right," he replied playfully.

"A MAID! Boy, you crazy. You can't have no maid in jail."

"I am at home at the condo, sis. I got out late yesterday. You know they can't keep a playa down for too long," Keyshawn explained.

"WHAT?! YESTERDAY?! And you're just now calling? Mama's gonna kill you Keyshawn Watson. She's been over her walking new tracks in the carpet, wondering if them folks down there did something to you."

"Look, sis, I had so much on my mind and had been through so much, my body shut down last night. This shit is crazy, and as crazy as it may seem, I think I'm going to come through it okay," he said, really feeling his chances were good.

"Have you talked to Auntie P yet?" she asked, talking in code like he'd taught her.

"Naw, sis. I haven't really spoken with anyone at all. I'm telling you, if it wasn't in a dream, we weren't talking," he replied.

Keysha was so happy her brother had made it home from jail; being a twin was different for her. She seemed to feel all the pain he felt at times. They had always been close and she hated the years their mother had sent him away, but even so, they'd talked almost every day, keeping up with what each other was doing.

Keyshawn had been proud of Keysha. She could have been so many things if she'd used the same excuses he did, but instead she'd used her head and wanted to get an education. He was glad one of the decisions he'd made before all this happened was to set up a fund that paid for her first four years in school. He didn't want her or their mother worrying about how things were going to get done. Keyshawn was going to make sure someone in the family had the opportunity to become something and make something of her life.

"Well, I'm at mom's crib, and I think you should make your way on over here," she said.

"Yeah, that's real talk; I'm about to get dressed in a minute. You know these people fucked my crib up. The condo association sent me a letter saying I have to move as well. It's all good though. Let me shower and get myself together so I can come over there."

"Okay; I'll start breakfast now."

"I'm on my way then. By the way, how is our daddy doing?" Keyshawn asked, shocking his sister.

~ ❖ ~

Keyshawn caught another taxi from his Condo out to Mitchell Field Airport to get a car to drive. He had a connection at Avis Rental who didn't sweat him as long as he dropped him an extra hundred under the table. As he pulled off in the black Chrysler 300 and headed back on the freeway toward the inner city, he couldn't help thinking about the last words Keysha had said to him before she hung up the phone about their father not having long to live. Keyshawn thought about how he'd treated Tim the last time he saw him and knew he was wrong. At first, when he was on top of the world, he really thought he couldn't care less if Tim lived or died, but he knew that wasn't the case at all. Now he really wanted to see his old man and have a conversation with him, look into his eyes, and grant him the forgiveness he knew he wanted. It would be the one thing Keyshawn did right if he didn't do anything else.

Chapter 8 ~

Li Chan sat in the Fox Point condo rubbing her stomach. She could now feel the new life of her unborn child growing inside of her and it made her smile. As beautiful and smart as she was, Li had never pictured her life taking the turns it had taken over the last several months. She knew her family would look at her with shame, but for some reason, the very fact that would have bothered her a year ago didn't bother her anymore.

Her father was big on the Japanese culture and her mother went along with whatever he said. It was the way things worked in the Chan household. Li Chan knew nothing about the American ways of living until she went to college in Ohio. Her college roommate was an African American girl from Atlanta, Georgia, who partied five nights a week and still made the Dean's List. Li learned to accept people and love them for who they were, not what color or culture they came from.

Keyshawn Watson was no different to her. When Li Chan took the assignment, she knew the department had stereotyped him because he was an African American—the way the Government thought the black man was the only race that stooped as low as they could to manipulate their own women and use them to make an income, having them sell their bodies for profits. When in actuality, her own culture dealt with a tradition they called geisha. It was really no different than the pimp game Keyshawn played.

There was something different about Keyshawn Watson, and Li Chan had known it from the first moment she laid eyes on him at the gas station. He had something soft and genuine lodged inside his pupils, like he had been here on earth before and was way ahead of his time. Still she didn't know it would lead up to where she was now. There was no denying she loved him more than anything else in the world.

Li silently thanked T.A. for having the conversation with Keyshawn that eventually led them to the bedroom. When he'd touched her, it was like magic happened in her heart. She instantly felt the passion from someone she was already admiring, who'd made her love boil over. Keyshawn had started out a little rough with her, and when he finally told her why, she'd understood he was just doing what he thought needed to be done to prove she was who she said she was. After a few minutes in, he'd relaxed and made love to her, not like a woman of the night or some whore he worked, but like a woman he loved. It might have all been in her imagination, but somehow things had taken the course she'd hoped they would take.

Li Chan had never felt so complete before she met Keyshawn Watson. She had never before thought making love could feel so special. She hated it had all come about the way it had, putting the rest of her life and career in jeopardy. Li felt in hindsight, she would do it all over again if it was with Keyshawn Watson.

She touched her stomach again and remembered she had a doctor's appointment in about an hour. She knew SAIC Bender would probably be looking for her by now. He was going to be shocked when she called him later today and handed in her walking papers. It was too risky for her to hang around the Bureau knowing Bender would investigate the Bennis incident to the fullest. Li Chan had already gathered enough information for Keyshawn to initiate his next plan. She hoped it would also keep him from dealing with other women, having them sell their bodies. She loved him dearly and wanted him to reach his goal of becoming a millionaire, and she was sure he could do it.

Li hadn't called him since he'd got out because she wasn't sure what all Daley had been up to. If he was clever enough to put a tracking device on her car, which she'd found in the front wheel well, he might have recorded some of their conversations. But she missed his voice and really couldn't wait much longer to hear from him. She picked up her throwaway phone and dialed the number for his sister.

Keyshawn pulled into his mother's driveway and exited the vehicle, looking around. He was still being cautious, making sure there was no tail on him. He knew the Feds didn't like being outdone and they would be on him like white on rice. The morning air smelled good and he looked up, viewing the clear skies.

He used the spare key his mother demanded he keep to let himself in. The smell of French toast and warm butter danced a slow dance with his nostrils, reminding him that was his sister's specialty. When he walked in the kitchen, his mother was sitting there with a cup of coffee, looking sadly out the back window into her yard.

"Why you looking so sad?" he asked.

"Oh my goodness," she said smiling, looking at her son then at Keysha who hadn't told her anything.

"You knew your brother was home, didn't you? I should put you both over my knee," she continued, standing up to wrap her arms around her baby. "Let me look at you, Keyshawn. Them people didn't go upside your head, did they?" she asked, concerned about his safety. Police brutality wasn't anything new and people were scared for their loved ones when they got arrested in the ghetto.

"Dang, ma, I was only in there for a second," he replied, hugging her back.

"It only takes a second. You see what just happened to that young man in the back of that ambulance."

"I know, but my lawyer was on top of everything. I was fine and I'm going to be fine. Now what's taking this girl so long with that French toast?" He asked, laughing.

They sat down to eat breakfast and Keyshawn filled his family in on what was going on and what he was charged with. He explained they didn't have much on him but he figured he and T.A. would lose the club in the process. His mother asked him about his friend and he told her it wasn't looking as good for T.A. due to a witness they had cooperating against him.

His mother started to bring up his father until the phone in Keysha's pocket started ringing. The twins looked at each other; they knew it could only be one person calling that number. Their mother started to say something to both of them; she didn't want Keysha involved in anything, but she knew that was going to be a useless argument.

Keysha passed her brother the phone and he excused himself from the table for a minute. Li Chan was excited to hear it was him who answered.

"Hey, king," she said anxiously.

"Hey, baby girl; you all right?" he replied, wondering where she was.

"I'm good, just being careful. A lot's going on and I want to make sure when this is all over with we're good," Li Chan said.

"I know what you mean, but we should be fine thanks to you," Keyshawn replied, making her feel she was worth her weight in gold.

"Meet me at the Fox P spot in a couple of hours; we need to catch up. I have to go see the doctor now, but I'm looking forward to seeing you," she murmured provocatively.

"Same here, baby. I'll be there," he replied, ending the call.

Chapter 9 ~

SAIC Bender had been around the block many times before. When he couldn't sleep through the night, he knew that was a sign things weren't adding up to him. The Watson case had been bothering him more than any other case he'd ever worked detail on. He tossed and turned, thinking no one as dirty as Keyshawn Watson should come out smelling as clean as he smelled right now.

The case should have been a slam-dunk, and Keyshawn Watson, like his partner T.A. Smith, should have been getting ready to spend at least thirty years in a federal prison for his crimes. Now the same case that was so strong had suddenly took a left turn and become weak. Bender realized the Government stood a chance of losing outright in the Watson matters. He knew if this happened, it would also affect him. There had been too much money spent on traveling to different cities and too many man-hours for things just to be a flop. Someone had to take responsibility. It didn't work like that and Bender knew it.

He got out his bed and walked in his kitchen again for the fourth time to go over the statement in the file Agent Bennis had given. The Bureau's computer techs had gone back four years tracking Bennis's movements on the Bureau's computers and nothing had popped up negative assuming foul play against the agent. Maybe a porn site or two he'd looked at, but Bender knew for a man of Bennis's caliber that was the norm. He wasn't married and didn't have any children. His file said he was an orphan who'd spent most of his young life going from group home to group home. Bennis was a four-point student all through high school and college, finishing on the Dean's List at Howard University.

It seemed as if this man's whole life had been dedicated to his work, so it bothered Bender tremendously why he would log on to a traceable file and delete information that was being used to incriminate Watson and Smith. When Bender had his worker's financials checked, everything there looked normal as well. Most agents who went bad usually had some type of money issues or some type of gambling problems. Bender had even run across a few cases where agents had gotten in bed with the mob because of debts they'd accrued gambling. But all of Agent Bennis's credit cards had small limits and none of them had been maxed out, so he wasn't in any financial trouble as far as Bender could tell. Somehow Bender had wholeheartedly known that would be the case.

SAIC Bender showered and dressed for the day. He dreaded going into the office at times like this. His phone would be ringing off the hook the moment he walked in. The mayor, the chief in command, hell, he wasn't sure if the president of the United States wouldn't be calling him to rip him a new asshole. Bender looked in the mirror as he straightened out his tie, trying to perfect the knot.

Li Chan had been on his mind as well. She was one of the Agency's best agents and it was unfortunate that illness was plaguing her from doing her job. Bender still didn't understand why she hadn't checked in with him after she'd left the hospital. He would make sure to see her as soon as he walked in.

He pulled up in the garage and parked in his spot. As soon as he walked in, he saw Agent Love waiting on him. Agent Love had spent most of the day yesterday talking to the doctors at the crazy home where one of Keyshawn Watson's girls was. It was a shame they knew Keyshawn was responsible for the condition the young lady was in, but again, they had no proof. It seemed to Bender that Keyshawn was steadily making slips through every crack.

As soon as he sat down, he had a conversation with Love; the girl at the hospital was going to be useless. It was clear Keyshawn was going to be a free man. Now they had to focus on Smith, who Bender was sure wasn't going to crack and take a deal to tell anything that he knew. It was a shot in the dark, but one thing about the Federal Government was they would sacrifice to get what they wanted.

Bender summoned for Agent Chan, needing to talk to her and find out if she was feeling any better. When he tried to locate her, she wasn't anywhere in the building. He tried to call her cell and voicemail picked up right away, meaning the phone was powered off. Bender left her a message asking her to call him right away when she was available. He hoped she was okay since he had no knowledge of the outcome of the hospital evaluation.

It wasn't five minutes after he'd hung up from leaving Li Chan a voicemail that his phone began ringing. The first call he'd taken was from the chief commander, wanting to know what had gone wrong in the Watson situation. SAIC Bender tried to explain the details to his boss the best he could, attempting to avoid the important stuff about the wire taps. He knew he couldn't elude from it too long, knew by the tone in the boss' voice he already had firsthand information on the whole case.

Only thing, Bender wasn't completely convinced Agent Bennis was the culprit who'd erased the wiretaps. His head said the evidence was indisputable, but his heart was telling him differently. That's what was making it a hard one to swallow. One of the rules in the Bureau was no one was to ever share a password to their secure logon and his man didn't seem the type to break that rule. It was a mistake a rookie would make, and it was also grounds for immediate termination if a person was caught.

By the time the conversation was over with the chief, Bender was told he had to fire Agent Bennis immediately, ending the call.

~ ~

Keyshawn jumped in the rental car thinking the moment he'd always dreaded had finally come. He pulled off heading in the direction of the hospital where his father was being treated. In his heart, he'd always loved his father, but he'd never respected the man who'd fathered two children then abandoned them. Thinking about that made him think maybe that was the reason his mindset was so fucked-up about his own unborn child. The baby inside of Li Chan's womb was definitely his, but he knew he didn't care if she had the baby or not.

He pulled into the visitor parking lot, making sure this was what he really wanted to do: look this man in the eye, knowing he had the same features as the coward who'd left his mother and sister to starve. If it wasn't for his grandmother's words, he knew he would have ultimately wished the cancer would take the man from the earth so he'd never have to set eyes on him again.

A cute little receptionist was at the front desk playing on her cellphone when he walked in. Keyshawn cleared his throat so she would look up and notice he was waiting to be helped. When she finally unglued her eyes from texting, she told him the room number and gave Keyshawn a visitor's pass. When he walked in the room and saw his father laying there, a different emotion came over him right away. Seeing the man who'd given him life helpless and almost out of breath made Keyshawn realize the value of life is priceless.

His father looked up and closed his Bible when he saw who had come through the door. His aging face quickly displayed a smile and his light brown eyes almost shined, as if he'd been given new life. "Come in, son," he said.

A day ago, Keyshawn would have snapped if this man had called him son. "Is it all right if I take a seat right here?" Keyshawn asked, sliding a chair close to the bed.

"Of course; I was just doing a little reading. You know what they say 'bout folks—we sure know how to find the Lord when we're in trouble."

"I hear ya," Keyshawn replied.

"I'm glad you came, Keyshawn. I know you don't like me one bit, son, and really, I can't blame you. What I did was wrong, and I'm learning more and more that we, as men, can't fix our wrongs by ourselves. Our egos are too big and we have too much pride in our hearts to ever admit when we mess up."

Keyshawn just listened as he talked; he couldn't stop staring at the man. It was like his hate had been so strong over the years, he'd never noticed that he was actually the spitting image of his father. If he could remove the damage the cancer was doing to him, it would have been like looking in the mirror.

"Son, I got out there bad on them drugs and I was chasing a high. I always loved you and your sister more than either of you would ever know, but that monkey will make you chose wrong every time."

"But why?" Keyshawn asked. "You had a good woman who worked her tail off to hold things down," he continued, almost sounding like when he was about nine, questioning his mother about his father.

"That's something I'll never be able to explain. I could use the excuse I'm only human, but I've also learned human beings know right from wrong. All I know is I messed up and I'm looking for forgiveness. Even if you never forgive me, son, I hope the Lord sees fit to forgive me."

At that very moment, Keyshawn wanted to forgive his father. He wanted to cry and tell his father he wanted to start all over because he had come to the realization he had a different monkey on his back. He wanted to get in the game to support his mother and sister, take care of his family like a man should, but he realized the deeper he'd gotten involved, the more it had become about the power and the love of money. He was no different than the man dying in front of him. He had a choice just as his father had.

"You know what, Pops? It may be a little too late to shoot buckets and build model cars, but I forgive you," Keyshawn said. He saw the smile crease his father's lips and that sent a warm bolt through him. "I hope you're around to see your grandchild," Keyshawn said.

"You got a child on the way, huh?" he asked.

"Yeah, it's a fucked-up situation, but a Watson is coming out of it."

"Listen, Keyshawn, no matter how bad the situation may be, life is only given by God, and if He sees fit to bless you and your lady with a life, that means He sees a future for that life. Your job is to manifest what He gives you into a good person."

Keyshawn never thought he would hear his father talk the way he was talking now. It almost sounded like he was back in Mississippi, sharing a piece of his favorite cake at the kitchen table with his grandmother.

"I feel ya on that, Pops, but I didn't mean to make a baby. I got in some trouble—"

His father stopped him mid-sentence raising his hand. He didn't let Keyshawn finish what he was going to say before interrupting him. "I'm going to tell you this, Keyshawn, and you take it for what it's worth. God makes no mistakes, son, and His plan is the only plan that counts. We may alter it or try to go around it, but in the end, He will have it His way," he said with a very serious look on his face.

Keyshawn thought for a second. He didn't know when his father had become so big on God, but he liked the change in him. So many thoughts flooded Keyshawn's mind listening to his father speak. It wasn't the first time in his life he'd thought about totally walking away from the game, but something kept pulling him toward the million-dollar goal he'd set—making him feel he wasn't an accomplished man if he stopped short of what he'd set out to do.

His father had never told him he'd seen his case on the news and read about what his son was doing in the newspaper. That wasn't important to Tim at the moment. The only thing he cared about was telling his son he loved him and he wanted to make amends for being a lousy father. Tim felt deep down, looking into his eyes, his goal had been accomplished. He lay in his hospital bed feeling like a ton of bricks had been lifted from his heart.

Tim reached and gave Keyshawn the Bible he had been reading every day, placing it in his son's hand. "If you have a problem and need answers, everything is right in here, son. If you can't find the answers in this book, there is no problem."

Keyshawn had heard those same words from his grandmother and figured maybe there was a little truth to what he was hearing. He wasn't sure he was ready to go that far in discovering what the answers were, but he knew he had problems to deal with. He started to say something to his father and noticed his eyes were closed. Key thought at first they must have given him some type of pain medicine that had made Tim sleepy.

As he stood up, five people in white coats rushed into his father's room. Keyshawn was so preoccupied with hearing his father speak, he hadn't noticed the heart-monitoring machine Tim was connected to had flatlined.

"Excuse us, sir. We're going to have to ask you to step out the room," one of the doctors said.

"What the fuck you talking about? Wake him up so we can finish talking!" Keyshawn demanded.

"I'm sorry, sir. He's gone."

BOOK TWO

Chapter 10 ~

The line of cars wasn't that long headed to Ebenezer Baptist Church on Martin Luther King Drive. Keyshawn, his mother, and his sister rode in the limo, and a few of his friends along with one of his daddy's cousins trailed them to the service. Key looked out the window as they neared the church and thought about all the times he'd wished death on Tim for not being there to support him or the family.

Now that Tim was gone, he missed having a father. It made him think about his own unborn child in Li's stomach. He really didn't care about having a child at first, especially with her, but now that he'd lost his own father, something inside him made him respect the life that was coming. The baby would be a part of him and Tim. For a quick moment, he smiled, hoping she would give him a son.

The limo pulled into the circular driveway of the church and Pastor Saffold was standing in front of the glass double doors, waiting to greet the family. He wasn't that familiar with Tim because Tim wasn't a member of the church, but he'd gone to the hospital to see him per Keyshawn's mother's request.

Keysha was a nervous wreck as the service began and the pastor delivered a powerful sermon on going home to be with the Lord. He spoke on how he'd gone to see their father and he was sure Tim was in a much-better place. He touched Keyshawn when he said, as he looked directly at him, how Tim had told him he wanted nothing more than for his son and daughter to have a life without perversity.

Key wrapped his arms around his sister's shoulders, offering what little comfort he could. He looked over at his mother as the choir started singing *Take Me Back, Dear Lord*, and he hadn't seen her look so at peace since he'd gotten her the new house. Maybe death wasn't really that bad after all, he thought. One thing T.A. use to tell him was the only thing a person was born with was a death certificate. He knew as harsh as it sounded it was true. None of the glamour and fame, the jewelry and fancy whips could go with you in the ground when you died. *'What was it all for?'* he thought. Life had to be more than the power and currency he craved so badly.

Key looked behind him when he felt a tap on his shoulder. When he turned around, he was surprised to see Li Chan sitting there in a black dress. She no longer looked like a cheap hoe or a federal agent to him. She looked like the woman who was having his baby. He touched her hand as the pastor finished up and the pallbearers carried his father out to the car that would be delivering Tim to his final resting spot.

At the cemetery, Pastor Saffold said a few more words about Tim before the small crowd chose flowers, removing them from the top of Tim's money-green casket. It was hard for Key to hold his sister up on her feet. Her knees were weak and she sobbed uncontrollably asking the Lord, "Why my father?" He whispered to his twin everything was going to be all right. Keysha cried on his tuxedo jacket, soiling the suede pelts, but Keyshawn didn't care about that. He tightened his arms around her, hugging her while she let it all out, hugging her brother back.

"You're all we have left, Keyshawn, and I'm worried about you," Keysha said.

"Don't worry, sis; I got this. I think some things are going to be a lot different around here," he replied, thinking about the money T.A. had left for him.

"I hope so. I couldn't take not having you in my life," she replied.

Keyshawn knew exactly how his family felt about him; they all were close-knit. Throughout all the trials and tribulations, the three of them were really all they had. He looked at his mother and saw the tears flowing from her eyes as they lowered the casket. Key knew he had the strongest mother in the world. She had endured many aches and pains dealing with Tim; so many, she hadn't trusted in another man since he'd left them. But something told Keyshawn as he watched her that her love had never died for his father, despite what he'd put her through. He was just hoping she wouldn't break down when no one was around.

Keyshawn rode with Li Chan after leaving the cemetery. He knew they were having a little gathering at his mother's, and he told Bone and Big Daddy to go over there and watch after his family for him. He wasn't sure if he could take much more himself. He was glad he had such down-ass partners who didn't mind looking out.

SAIC Bender was livid as he sat at his desk reading the resignation of Agent Li Chan. How could she do this to him in the middle of an ongoing investigation? He knew she was sick, but whatever it was, if she needed time off, she could have just as easily requested it, and he would have made sure she got the time needed with pay.

He had so much going on and it was all falling apart on him. As a civilian, Agent Li Chan didn't have to testify against Keyshawn Watson and that also made no sense to him. He figured if she wanted to quit, at least she could have waited until the case was over. She, too, had put in hard work and labored to bring this criminal to justice.

He rocked back in his chair, closing his eyes. Bender wished he could actually wake up and be on Mars; maybe outer space would be a better place for him right now. He had one dead agent, one agent who'd botched wire taps, and now one who'd quit in the middle of a case. None of it was looking good to him. He knew his superiors were going to have his asshole turned inside out.

"Why now, Li?" he said to himself. "What in the world would make an agent want to let a man go free?" he continued, thinking out loud.

Suddenly he had a thought about his last thought. "What in the world would make an agent want to let a man go free?" SAIC Bender had to think of the gender differences, and the fact that Keyshawn Watson had to have something special. He hoped, just because his other women hadn't turned on him, he was wrong about the notion that crossed his mind. *'Naw,'* he thought, *'it was impossible.'* But as impossible as it might have seemed, he had to start checking it out right away. He picked up his phone and dialed Agent Love's number. When Agent Love answered, he ordered him to find Li Chan and put a tail on her right away.

Chapter 11 ~

"You have a collect call. To accept this call, press one," the operator's voice came through the receiver, and Suzy put the baby down to take her man's call. She was shocked at what Jamal had asked her to do the last time they'd spoken, but she knew she would do anything to get her baby-daddy out of the House of Corrections.

"Hey, you do what I asked and get that information together for me?" Jamal asked.

"Yes, I got it, baby," she replied.

"Good, now I want you to click over on the three-way and call that cop dude. What was his name again?"

"The newspaper said his name was Special Agent Bender."

"Yeah; when he hears what we have to say, I'm sure that little news will get me back to the bricks and lovin' on you, girl," Jamal said, making his baby-mama's pussy wet with the thought of him being home.

On her last visit, she had listened closely to everything the girl in the booth next to her was saying to her boyfriend. At first, it was really unbelievable to think that the girl's brother was a big-time drug dealer who had a federal agent pregnant. When she got home and saw the ten o'clock news with the standoff of a man and the police, she had known the information she'd heard was true. The news showed the agent as they interviewed her about what had gone down when she'd shot the suspect in the house.

Jamal was trying everything he could to get close to the dude named Brandon, but it wasn't easy. Brandon was a stay-to-himself type of guy, and the only time he mingled with the other inmates was on the basketball court during recreation. Now he didn't need to get close to Brandon. He had heard a few of the other inmates talking about Key and another dude by the name T.A. during domino games. Jamal had never really paid too much attention to jailhouse talk because most of the young niggas in there were wannabe gangsters anyway.

Jamal had heard Key owned a nightclub and was moving major weight on the weed side. Everybody talked about his Benz and one young nigga was even in there boasting he was his driver. Everyone knew that wasn't true because that particular dude was in there locked up for grand theft-auto.

Jamal listened as the phone rang several times and Bender's voicemail picked up. He left Bender a message about who he was and that he had some pertinent info for him regarding the Watson case. If nothing else, Jamal knew hearing the last name Watson was going to get the attention of the agent. One thing he did was read the newspaper every day, and he'd seen on the front page of the *Metro* where a man expected of human trafficking had walked from federal holding. The article had said, due to missing evidence, the government's case was weak. Jamal had a pretty good idea about what had happened to the evidence against Keyshawn Watson.

Keyshawn rode on the passenger side of Li Chan's personal Impala. They were headed to the apartment he'd had Big Daddy secure for Venus and T.A's two girls. He knew both of T.A's people were leaving town tomorrow, so they would be gone by the time for him to make his next court appearance. Venus was facing a maximum of five years for the credit card charges, but she was holding out like a real ride-or-die bitch.

"So how does it feel to be a civilian now?" Keyshawn asked as they pulled to a light on Holton Street.

"I don't know really, but it feels like I made the right choice. You know I thought I would never give up the job, but when I looked into your eyes one day, I couldn't help but fall in love with you," Li replied.

"So you're in love, huh?" Key said, reaching over touching Li's stomach.

"I'd sure say so," she smiled.

Li had been very lonely emotionally for some years now. Dating just wasn't something she wanted to get into. It was strange because she knew over half the men she worked with all had small crushes on her. Sometimes she was intrigued by it and wished one of them had the balls to ask her on a date. Even if she would have refused the offer, it still would have been nice if one of them had tried his luck. When she first faked her move like she was going out on a date for Keyshawn to make his money, she'd wished she was going to see a man and the man she was going to see was him. She sometimes pulled over in a secluded area and masturbated thinking about Keyshawn and her making love.

Bender had never wanted to give her more than two grand to take back, but she had persuaded him she needed more and more every time. She'd told him the other girls were bringing in more money, and if she didn't step her game up, he was probably going to replace her. Each time the purses got bigger, and she smiled every time she filled out a slip to get the money from the federal fund. It was all she could do at the time to secretly take care of the man she was in love with.

They both got out and Key rung the bell since he didn't have a key to the place. Venus' voice came over the intercom system, asking who it was and he replied it was daddy. She held onto the buzzer, making sure he was in the building. When they walked in, Key was glad to see the place had been nicely-furnished for the girls. He loved Big Daddy for being such a real nigga.

"Hey, daddy, we 'bout to get back to work?" Venus asked, ready to start making moves and chasing the paper for her pimp.

"Naw; we got to hold up. There's entirely too much going on, and if we continue right now, we gonna all end up under the jail," Keyshawn replied.

He watched Venus' facial expression get long with disappointment, and he truly loved the fact that his bottom-bitch was ready to get back at his paper. He thought about the information Li Chan had given him and knew Venus was excellent at pulling the credit card schemes. But as bad as he wanted to reach his million-dollar goal, something inside of him was telling him to hold up for a minute and wait to see his next hand. Keyshawn was going to have to play the hand he was dealt. His full house had already been beat; now he knew, if he wanted to play the next hand, he had to be drawing at a royal flush. Otherwise, it might be the end of him, and he would be out the game for good.

T.A's girls were already packed and ready to be dropped off at the train station. It was too risky for them to fly out because the Feds were usually in the airports looking for anyone or anything that looked suspicious. Key reached in his pocket and took out a wad of bills, instructing Venus on what to do with the girls. She assured him his orders would be carried out just as he explained them to her.

Venus shot Kimmie a look, but it wasn't the evil look of a jealous wife-in-law, but one of sure gratitude. She knew, if it weren't for Kimmie, they would have never been in this mess, but also if it weren't for her, they would have never gotten out of it either. They made eye contact before Venus stepped to her. Li Chan didn't know what to expect until Venus hugged her and told her she loved her.

Keyshawn and Li got back in the car heading for the freeway toward the Fox Point location. They hadn't had a real moment to talk and get caught up on everything Li Chan had to fill him in on.

"So what happened at Tiahmo's place?" Key asked.

"It was all bad, baby. First of all, when we killed Daley, I left them to dump the body on the other end of the park. They just so happened to pick a spot where two kids were making out and saw them," Li said.

"That's fucked up."

"Tell me about it. When I heard what was happening, I saw our life flash in front of us for a second time. I knew I had to do something, so I showed up at the scene and talked my boss into letting me play negotiator," she laughed.

"Damn, baby, I think I taught you too much," Keyshawn replied, laughing back.

"Seriously though, there was no way I could leave him alive, baby. I hope you're not mad at me for killing your friend."

"Hell, naw; it was like you said—either our asses or his. You did exactly what you had to do," Key replied, giving her his unyielding focus now.

Li Chan left out the fact she'd called Keysha to help her with the little charade. She knew she shouldn't have, but she also knew she could cross that bridge when she came to it—*if* she ever came to it.

"Hey, you never told me about the Paris girl. You know Bender found her out at the mental complex all fucked up," Li said, exasperated.

"I made the mistake of not having her killed. The more I think about what Natty is doing to T.A., I feel like I should have had the dude just off her," Keyshawn said.

"Well, in her case, baby, I don't think it will be necessary for you to worry too much. Whatever your guy did was final enough. I saw the doctor's reports, and they said she's permanently damaged for the rest of her life."

"I'm glad I don't have to worry about that dumb bitch. I mean all I did for her and she went behind my back trying to get with another nigga," Key said.

Keyshawn wasn't a sucka. He would have accepted the rules of the game if Paris had just got knocked by another playa. But what she'd done was unacceptable. She was out for revenge, and just so happened to be with the people responsible for killing his best friend and making an attempt on his life. He couldn't sit back and let that ride.

They pulled into the condo and parked in the garage. Keyshawn hadn't been there since he'd been home, and he figured he would probably just move his stuff in since he had to leave his place. When they walked in, things looked exactly the same as they had the last time they were there.

"Look in the front closet, honey," Li said as she made her way to the bathroom.

"What? Another surprise?" he replied, opening the front closet door. Keyshawn saw Li had gone shopping for him. She'd picked out a few jogging suits and some jean outfits that were his style. When she came from the bathroom, she didn't look like she had when she'd gone in.

"Damn, baby, you look good," Key said.

"If I look that good, why you still got that choirboy outfit on?" she replied provocatively.

"Wait a minute; who's the pimp here?" he playfully said, guiding her to the bedroom.

The first time they made love had been the highlight of her life, she thought. Li Chan's body had been total oblivious to what passion felt like. When Keyshawn put his dick inside her, she'd begun instantly building toward a state of new resolve and had fallen in love with him. This time was no different. Key was much slower and much gentler with her as he kissed her ear like it was her second Gspot. She felt her body respond to him as her pulse accelerated.

"I love you, daddy," Li said as she felt his thick, long dick penetrate her pussy lips.

Keyshawn loved the way Li Chan felt. It was like she was untainted and her body truly belonged to him. Cautiously, he turned her over on her side, not wanting to put too much pressure on her stomach, protecting his unborn child. Li lifted her leg, using her natural agility to place it around his legs, while he slid in and out of her wetness, causing her to moan with pleasure.

She wanted to fuck! She wanted him to make her feel like tonight was the night she got retribution for all the lonely nights she'd spent masturbating, playing with herself. A passage she'd read in college by Leonardo da Vinci played in her mind as Keyshawn held her hips between his hands. "The art of procreation and the members employed therein are so repulsive, that if it were not for the beauty of the faces and the adornments of the actors and the pent-up impulse, nature would lose the human species."

Keyshawn thought for a brief moment it had been a long time since he'd actually made love to a woman. In fact, it was Quesha who had been the person. Something about the feeling Li Chan gave him made him realize he'd missed the feeling of monogamous passion himself. He had become so focused on the rules of the game he'd forgotten he was even human.

Li could feel Keyshawn's dick get harder and thicker as his thrusts became more powerful. "Come on, daddy; fuck this pussy. This is your pussy," she cried out.

Her words made him feel even more enticed as he started pulling her backwards into him, making sure she covered every inch of his flesh with her flesh. He felt his body getting ready to explode and pulled her in totally, becoming one with her as his juices shot inside her.

Li Chan lay there in a fetal position with Keyshawn still behind her, holding on to her. Her scent smelled really fresh as he stroked her silky hair. There had to be a means to an end, he thought. What more could a man want? He had a little money and a down-ass chick who was willing to die for him. Keyshawn made up his mind at that very moment he was through. He was going to get completely out the game. If Big Daddy could do it and live well, so could he. He was about to let four words come out his mouth he never thought he would say to any woman.

Chapter 12 ~

SAIC Bender woke up to his cell phone ringing. He checked the clock on the nightstand and saw it was an hour earlier before he would have liked to be awake. When he looked at the caller display, he saw the incoming call was from Agent Love, who he had looking for ex-agent Li Chan. He hoped like hell Love had some information for him.

"Hello; this better be good," Bender said in a groggy tone.

"Not really, boss. I've been staked at her apartment all day and night, and there is no sign of this chick. I've seen people going in and out the building, but no one who remotely resembles Li Chan," Love replied.

"Well, check all the flight manifests and every possible way of traveling a person could think of. There's no fucking way this broad vanished into thin air."

"Roger that, boss. Did you want me to stay on detail here as well when I finish?" Agent Love asked.

"I don't see a need. She couldn't possibly know I suspect some type of foul play, but if she isn't coming home, she's somewhere. Check the last known address for that Watson guy, flash a photo or two of her, and see if anyone's seen her around there in the last couple of days."

"Okay, I'm on top of it," Agent Love said before ending the call.

Bender figured he might as well get up and get his day started. He had a nine o'clock appointment with ex-agent Bennis. Something was telling Bender that Bennis recently had some interaction with Li Chan. Bender calculated each movement Li Chan had made since day one. He was trying to figure out when and if she'd gone bad, how and why had it happened.

He thought about the first time she'd come back to the division needing more money to fake off a higher-profile clientele; nothing was registering there. Then he thought about how she'd showed up on the scene when they discovered Daley's killer. Bender thought Li Chan was supposed to be looking into a matter regarding another human trafficking case in Chicago, but everything had been moving so fast, it had slipped his mind until last night.

If she was dirty, he knew he wouldn't hesitate to slap murder charges on her for the shooting of Daley's murder. Her story added up when she'd filed her report and IA had brushed it off since the guy was responsible for the death of a federal agent. What really got Bender was how conveniently she became sick when it was time for her to testify against Keyshawn Watson. He knew if Li Chan was guilty, she would most likely spend the rest of her life in a federal prison.

It wasn't unheard of for a female to fall for the wrong guy. It made Bender think about the days when he was just a rookie and a bus heading to Milan Federal Institution wasn't able to make it. One of the prisoners had a handcuff key and a nine millimeter pistol. He end up shooting both the guards and escaping. When they finally caught the suspect, he'd told them a female guard he was having sex with had given him everything he needed to escape.

This was ten times worse than that case though. Ex-Agent Li Chan could possibly be tied to the murder of her own partner. That gave Daley an idea. He picked up the phone and called his office. The phone rang three times before Mary Beth, his personal assistant, picked up.

"Federal Bureau of Investigations, Special Agent Bender's office. How may I help you?" she said, not knowing it was the boss.

"Good morning, Mary. This is Bender. I'm going to need you to hold all my calls this morning. Also ex-Agent Bennis is coming in.

Tell him I will be running late and I would like him to stick around until I get there. Now patch me to the Forensic Unit, please," he demanded. His tongue was going so fast he didn't give her the chance to tell him about the message he had from some Jamal who was at the House of Corrections.

Bender knew Mike Parks well. They had worked in Dayton, Ohio, about four years ago, chasing down a serial killer. Mike had gotten promoted to handle the forensics in Milwaukee about three months before Bender caught his break.

"Forensics. Parks speaking."

"This is Bender. How's it going in the land of science?" he asked.

"It's going. Working some blood samples from your case as we speak," Parks replied.

"Good, but I need a favor, if possible," Bender asked.

"Anything for a Dayton boy. What you got?"

"I need a team ASAP to meet out by Daley's residence. Want to see if there's anything there that connects a certain person to some foul play," Bender replied, not wanting to give out too much information. News really travelled around the division, and he wanted to be sure of his thoughts before he smudged another agent's name. It was already enough going on that he didn't need any mistaken drama.

"Send over the address. I got several early birds here who wouldn't mind getting out their lab coats and hitting the field," Parks said.

"Good. I'll meet you and your team there." Bender disconnected the call.

He quickly dressed without showering or shaving yesterday's whiskers and grabbed all four files he had—Daley's, Chan's,

Bennis's, and Watson's. He tossed them in a briefcase, kissed his wife, and left out the door.

~ ❖ ~

Venus and Chrissy made sure T.A.'s people got on the train safely. They watched them head off, jumped back in the car, and rode through downtown for a while. Chrissy wanted to stop in the mall to pick up a few items and Venus thought it was a good idea. Neither of them knew they had a tail on them when they left the train station.

Inside the mall, they shopped at Lady Footlocker and Venus bought a black Dobb hat from a hat boutique for Keyshawn. She used one of the last credit cards she had from before she went to jail. The amount was too small to be traced, so she wasn't worried at all. Outside the store was an elderly gentleman who looked to be almost seventy. He was well-dressed, sitting on a bench, reading a paper. He looked at Chrissy with inviting eyes, and she looked right back at him. It was like her hoe-sense kicked into gear and all she saw was money.

Chrissy elbowed Venus and Venus thought about what daddy had said about the heat being on them. She let Chrissy know it wasn't a good idea.

"Ah hell, it won't hurt to just see what's up. Besides that shirt he has on looks like it cost a fortune," Chrissy said, not taking Venus seriously at all.

She approached the man sitting there and engaged in casual conversation for about three minutes. After Venus observed Chrissy place her hand on the man's right knee, which was their sign he was a legitimate mark. Venus knew there was no stopping her wife-in-law. They disappeared into the parking structure with Venus a few steps behind them. All the time, the federal agent who was watching them was snapping photos from his cell phone. After the agent gathered enough evidence, he went back inside the mall and stopped at the hat store. He showed his badge and got a copy of the transaction Venus had made.

Chapter 13 ~

Keyshawn sat at the table with his mother and his sister talking about what was going on. His mother was still a little nervous, hoping he wasn't going to have to go back to serve time in prison. Keyshawn didn't know what the outcome was going to be, but he knew the State's case was totally weak against him, and his lawyer said he had a good chance at getting probation. He wasn't totally convinced, but it was something he could go on and tell his family without lying to them.

Michele had made a big lunch and she was tired. Keyshawn and Keysha told her to go rest; they would clear the table. She hugged her daughter and kissed him on the cheek. They watched the greatest mother in the world walk off to her room to rest. When she was completely out of sight, they began washing the dishes and talking amongst themselves.

"So how is Brandon holding up?" Keyshawn asked.

"He's doing good. I'm supposed to go out there in a couple of hours to see him. I'll let him know you asked about him."

"I see that little nigga's a real dude. He held his weight like a player."

"Yeah, he's crazy about you. He thinks you're next to God, let him tell it."

Her comment made Keyshawn think about their father and their grandmother. Before the death of his father, he might have made a slick comeback and compared himself agreeing with Brandon's analogy of him, but Keyshawn knew game time was over. He had to step up even more on every level. Feeding his family was something he was going to do regardless.

"So how do you feel about Kimmie shooting Tiahmo?" Keysha asked.

The question caught him off-guard for a second. "I mean, shit, that was fucked-up, but I guess she had to do what she had to do. You know what I'm saying?" Keyshawn replied.

"Man, that nigga was crazy as fuck, wasn't he? To go into a standoff with all them damn police like that. If she hadn't killed him, they were going to kill him anyway."

"You're probably right. They knew what had gone down, so I kind of agree with you," Key said, putting the last plate in the cabinet.

"When I talked to that nigga on the phone, he sounded like he was gone off something a little stronger than weed," Keysha said.

"Wait a minute. What do you mean, when you talked to him on the phone?"

"I had called Kimmie's burnout looking for you because your crazy self hadn't called anyone to tell us you were locked up. When she answered, she was right in the thick of things with Tiahmo. I mean, he had guns blazing, talking about he was going to kill her and he wasn't going back to the joint—all types of crazy nonsense. So Kimmie put him on the phone and I told him what the dealio was with her. I guess that's how she was able to get the drop on him," Keysha explained, noticing a weird look spread across her big brother's face.

Keyshawn was livid with Li Chan. When they'd talked, that was one of the details she'd neglected to fill him on. He knew she knew he would snap. Involving his family in his street life was not an option for Keyshawn. He wanted to keep his mother and sister as safe from any harm as he could. If something was ever to happen to any one of them, he knew the city wouldn't be able to sleep. He wasn't going to stress his frustration in front of his sister, but now he felt Li Chan was doing a little too much.

"It's all good, Key," he said. They sometimes called each other Key. "Just from now on, I don't want you getting in the middle of anything," he continued.

She still sensed the heat, but she also could tell what he was saying to her was out of sure concern for her safety.

"You know you're probably right," she replied, wiping the top of the stove.

Keyshawn had put the disc he'd received from Big Daddy in a small safe he kept at his mother's house. He never really kept anything in there but about three grand for emergency money and his passport. He was glad he'd obtained one before any felonies hit his record. He removed the tape and went down in the basement where he'd put in a state-of-the-art system for Michele. The hundred-foot-wide Sony screen was the best money could buy. The Bose speakers mounted on the wall played crystal clear and made it seem like you were in a living room or at a Marcus Theatre.

Key grabbed the remote when he stuck the disc in and pressed 'play'. The tape came on like a motion picture with a white background and a king piece from a chess set. "Man, this nigga is something else," Keyshawn said aloud to himself.

"Hey, playboy. If you're watching this video, either one or two things have transpired. I'm either ten-toes-up or them people got me. Hopefully, it's just that them folks touched me and I can live to see another day. But on to what a nigga needs to say.

"I'm sure you got the money from Big Daddy 'cause he's a real nigga. That was some side money I was shaving from the club as a nest egg. It wasn't supposed to be known about until it hit three million—one a piece. Shit got crazy when we lost our other brother, but you know these streets are cold but fair. So if I'm ten-toes-up, just know I'm in a better place and don't go out there doing anything stupid. You're the last one left on the streets, lil bro, and the game needs you. That's what I made this tape for, the life of the game. I never told you, but one game of chess can last for five years if two people learn to counter moves wisely. That's about the life expectancy of this pimp game as well, my nigga.

"I made this tape right after you told me everything going on with the Kimmie bitch, and I wanted to say, bro, never take your eyes off the prize. You're a pimp. I saw it from day one. The shit is in you from the root of your soul, so continue to do pimp-shit like a true playa. I know you got that bitch knocked up, and I'm glad I'm going to be a godfather; that shit even sounds slick—godfather—but don't take anything for granted. Remember the game has eight pawns that are expendable. They're used to protect the king for as long as they're needed, but they're also used to put the king in position to escape danger, one move at a time.

"Well, young bro, I've got to go, but remember every player gets eight pawns, and also remember this: a pawn is just what it is—a fucking pawn. Your move, bro."

Keyshawn sank back into the couch and thought about what T.A. had just said. He also thought about the conversation he'd had with his sister and knew, as much as he cared for Li Chan, she was a loose cannon. Love had made her no better than Paris or Natty in a certain way. She was looking to keep a nigga, regardless of the price she had to pay. He knew he had a lot of thinking to do. T.A. would never steer him wrong and that was something he had to take into deep consideration. It was becoming clear Li Chan would most likely become a liability rather than an asset.

Keyshawn knew what he had to do. He removed his phone and dialed Venus' number. He had all the credit card information Li

Chan had given him and even had some extra knowledge she'd taken the time out to bless him with. He could elevate his game to the next level, and his bottom-bitch had the same potential as Li Chan. Except she wasn't exposed to people who could ruin everything the way Li Chan was.

Venus' phone went to voicemail so he tried it one more time. It wasn't like her not to answer his call. When the phone went back to voicemail, he left her a message to check-in right away. There was a serious message in what he'd just watched, and Keyshawn knew T.A. was telling him to stay on his grind but watch his back. He was right. He'd come up in a world where women were who they were and what they were. The game was in him and to change now would be undoubtedly a mistake.

His phone rang and he knew who it was even before he answered it. "Where you at, bitch?" Keyshawn asked, feeling like his old self again. "We're at the mall—well, I'm still here waiting on Chrissy."

"Waiting on Chrissy? I know that bitch ain't spending my money frivolously at a time like this!" he snapped.

"Nope, not at all. She met an old trick in the mall, and they went to a Howard Johnson's around the corner," Venus said.

She had never lied to Keyshawn since she'd been down with him. He and Quesha had saved her life as far as she was concerned, and for that, she was ever grateful. She would ride or die for her daddy.

Keyshawn's blood pressure shot though the roof when Venus told him what was going down. "Leave that bitch right now and head back to the house. I'm going to meet you there."

"Okay, daddy," she replied, starting the engine of the rental Dodge Avenger she was driving. Key had had enough with people who went too far and thought it was a game. He really couldn't take it anymore. Chrissy probably had good intentions, but bad things happened when you had good intentions but refused to follow orders. Keyshawn would have to deal with her the way he should have dealt with her a long time ago. He had too much to lose.

Chapter 14 ~

SAIC Bender, along with the forensic team from the FBI, went through Agent Daley's residence with a fine-tooth comb. Bender made sure he looked through the entire bedroom and every closet, looking for any evidence that might implicate Daley knew something about his partner Li Chan. Bender had always known Daley admired Li Chan as more than a partner. He was a man with two heads as well, so he would catch Daley looking at Chan in a strange way during briefings. His first mind had told him to separate them a year ago, but he only followed his first mind when it dealt with handling cases. Personal gut feelings had no merit to Bender.

So far the search of Daley's home was coming up empty, and he was left feeling stupid. Bender had just known pulling Parks and his men from the division wouldn't lead to a wild goose chase. It was just incredible to believe people like Watson could commit crimes and not leave behind any clues. Bender was stumped by the thought. The only thing Bender found was a sticky note attached to Daley's refrigerator. The note had Li Chan's name and last week's date written in red ink on it. The note also had a smiley face, with both the eyes made out of hearts. It was written on stationary paper that came factory dated.

A little embarrassed, Bender dismissed Parks. He told him he could take his boys back to the lab. Bender told Agent Parks he wanted to stick around for a little while longer and put Daley's place back in order like they'd found it. Parks shook his head as he looked at his long-time friend. He knew firsthand how the job was when it got the best of you. Agent Parks was just glad he was no longer behind the line of fire anymore. It was a lot less stressful being in the lab working with DNA samples than ducking bullets and canvassing crime scenes every day.

Bender sat at Daley's kitchen table for about thirty minutes, thinking. He got up and started putting everything back in its place, doing it even neater than they'd found it. When he was done, he stood by the front door looking back at Daley's home. Daley was sort of a slob, but you would never be able to tell by the way he dressed for work. His shirts were always white and lightly starched, and his slacks had nice creases in them. Before Bender left, he wanted to take one more look in Daley's closet at the rest of his attire.

He walked back into his dead agent's bedroom and opened the double wooden doors to the closet that stored his clothes. Something wasn't adding up as he scanned the garments. There were no more white shirts hanging up, and the only pants hanging in there was a pair of Adidas jogging pants.

Bender checked the pockets on the jogging pants and found another piece of stationary. This one was dated a day prior to the last one, but had the same smiley face and same heart-shaped eyes. Only difference was at the bottom he noticed the letters S.W.A.L.B.A.K.W.S. He had no idea what it meant, but it was surely Daley's handwriting.

He tucked that note inside his pocket with the other one and started closing the door, when he noticed a Nike shoebox that looked out of place. He bent down and opened the box and picked up the black wiring tangled up inside. Bender looked at it closely and knew it was wire casing used to harness a GPS tracking system. Daley must have been following somebody at one point, Bender thought. But the rest of the equipment was nowhere to be found as he checked a few other shoeboxes in the closet. He placed the wiring back in the box and took it with him.

"Daley, what were you fucking up to?" Bender said aloud to himself.

Bender got back in his car and picked up his cell phone. He called Mary Beth to see if Agent Bennis was still there at the division waiting. When she confirmed he was still sitting in the conference room patiently waiting, Bender disconnected the call giving his unmarked a listlessly heavy foot on the gas pedal. Another thought crossed his mind: *'Why would a guilty man be so cooperative?'* Agent Bennis might have been guilty of being a scapegoat, but he wasn't the one who'd tampered with the wire taps. Bender was almost a hundred percent sure. Again he was so in a rush, Mary Beth didn't get a chance to tell him about the possible informant who'd called and left a message on his voicemail.

Keyshawn had gone from feeling okay to having the worst headache he'd ever had in his life. So much seemed to be going on that it all seemed to be crashing down on him like a bulldozer knocking down a building. Just so happened all of the bricks fell on top of him. Keyshawn knew the game wasn't supposed to be all peaches and cream—it would have been ridiculous for him to believe that—but he also knew he would soon get things back to normal and better than they ever were. Key felt where there was a will there was a way. His grandmother use to always say that and he had always believed that. Even though she meant it to be taken as an affirmation to live a spiritual life, he was applying it to the life he lived.

That was what had propelled him that day when he arrived back in Milwaukee from Mississippi. He could have just as easily lain down and accepted the way his family was living, where they were living, and how they were barely making it, but he had a sure-will to change things, and pimping was his way. The drug game had its place, but it wasn't for him. The risk was far too great for the rewards, and he didn't want to take the chance of dealing with anyone who couldn't sleep in the same bed with him. Working a bitch had become the final destination—they were the will and he was the way.

But Key knew right now he really had to clean things up with his camp. He had to make sure when those people got him back in front of the judge, they wouldn't be able to take him from his throne. Every loose end he could think of had to be sewed up now. Keyshawn picked up his phone and dialed Bone. He had mad love for Bone because he knew Bone was one of the smart ones. Bone had had a short run as a Dboy and had once sold a piece of work here and there, but when his money got right, Bone took the time and perfected another gift—gambling.

Gambling, selling dope, or pimping—it didn't matter. Whatever you did in the streets to make your paper all came with what was called the gift and the curse. Key knew there were ups and downs to every element of survival, and Keyshawn knew only the strong survived. The weak had no choice but to wither away and die when their season was up. He was a four-season nigga, and it was high time he changed from fall to spring so the sun could shine again.

Bone agreed to meet him at Big Daddy's for a quick second so they could talk. That was one thing about Bone: he never talked on the phone about anything. He wasn't even a D-boy any longer but he still practiced D-boy principals. Keyshawn wanted to meet up with him because Bone had a connection with the one person who could do and handle things like Tiahmo. Key needed a killer with no remorse right now. He wasn't quite sure how far he was willing to go, but far enough to save his own ass—that he was sure of.

He pulled into the driveway of Big Daddy's club and saw the two-door navy blue Bentley coupe parked there. Big Daddy had just copped it a week ago and it was the prettiest muthafucka on the streets. There was another black Lincoln Town Car parked in front of Big Daddy's luxury whip. Keyshawn looked in the rearview mirror when he heard the loud music pull up behind him. He knew it was Bone. He was the only nigga who rode around playing eighties rap music on ten. Bone got out the car and headed to the passenger side of Keyshawn's rental. He got in and they slapped hands.

"Damn, I see Big Daddy stays in this muthafucka all day and night," Keyshawn said.

"The old man's making major moves, homie; that black Lincoln belongs to some nigga out here doing mortgages. I mean they say this nigga's making a hundred stacks a month on commission," Bone replied, knowing Big Daddy was going for a second club in Racine.

"A hundred a month? Shit, playa, we're both in the wrong business," Key said, doing the math in his mind.

"Tell me about it. So what's on your mind, fam? You ain't called a nigga because you changed your mind about gambling, I know." Bone smiled, looking through the few CD's Key had in the car.

"You know we lost our soldier T, so I wanted you to hook me up with your man Nick. I got a few loose ends I'm thinking need to be tied, playa."

"Say no more; I'll have 'em here tonight. As a matter of fact, he owes me a favor, so I know he'll be happy to come through and hear what you have to say."

"One, playa."

They slapped five, and Bone got out and back in his ride. Keyshawn heard the voice of The D.O.C. *It's Funky Enough* as Bone sped off. He was about to pull off, not wanting to interrupt Big Daddy during his meeting, although he would have liked to speak to him. But as soon as he had put the car in gear, he heard a voice calling him from the front entrance. It was Big Daddy, who must have seen him on the camera system.

"Neph, come in here for a second. I have somebody I want to introduce you to," Big Daddy said.

Keyshawn put the car back in park and got out. He walked in and followed Big Daddy straight to his office. When he stepped through the door, the cologne the man was wearing dazzled his nose because it smelled so good and fresh. Key had never smelled it before. His suit was tailored Armani and his pinky ring was better than Key's piece. When they say pinky rings cost about fifty, bling, bling, they weren't fucking kidding.

The dark-skinned brother had a low-fade cut, and if one didn't know better, he looked like something out of *Forbes* magazine. He politely stood up to shake hands with Keyshawn.

"Nice to meet you, brother. My name is Keith Swinson, CEO of K.S. Financial."

"I'm Keyshawn."

"I've heard a lot about you, my man. Your uncle here tells me you've got real potential to be a prime real estate owner. Owning property is where it is. You know there aren't too many things you can buy that increase in value once you take ownership of them," the well-dress man said.

"I heard that," Key replied, agreeing with the man.

In fact, it made him think. He really didn't know anything else he could buy that wouldn't lose value. Maybe that's why he'd become a pimp. He knew in his profession he didn't value anything anyway but the paper.

Chapter 15 ~

Key played the game very well. He stepped inside the Fox Point condo where Li Chan had been waiting on him to arrive. She was in the kitchen in her cloth robe, fixing some type of noodle dish that smelled really good. His first mind was to kick her in her ass for involving his sister in the bullshit, but he knew he had to use his head now, be real cool about things until it was all sorted out.

His goal at hand was to make Li Chan think that he was none the wiser. Keyshawn knew love was her angle, but even love could cost him a price he wasn't willing to pay. He wasn't going to make the same mistake T.A. had made with Natty. That was the thing about being a real nigga instead of a sucka. You were supposed to learn from other playas' mistakes and use what you learned to enhance your own style.

"Damn, that smells real good, baby," Key said, throwing his car keys on the mantle.

"Thank you. It's something we call Dan-Dan noodles," Li replied.

Keyshawn walked up behind Li Chan, rubbing her stomach, softly going underneath her robe searching for the heartbeat of his unborn child. Li's belly was starting to get a little pudgier from his growing seed dwelling inside her. Losing his father like he had, almost had a sentimental effect on Keyshawn, but that was when most players made their biggest mistake—going against the grain. It was like putting a single bullet inside a revolver and spinning the barrel, then pointing it at your own head. One of those times when you pulled the trigger you were going to get exactly what you weren't looking for. That's why Keyshawn had realized after watching the tape of his mentor and best friend—he couldn't go against the grain.

Li turned to kiss him and at first Key turned his mouth away so their lips wouldn't connect, but he thought about that move. He knew she was still sharp from her training and could possibly sense a change in his attitude if he wasn't careful. He created a sneeze then turned back to finish what she'd started. Li moaned with pleasure like a virgin experiencing her first passionate tongue-loving.

Keyshawn didn't want to get excited and kept letting his mind drift off while she caressed his body. He knew if he made love to her, she would only get deeper into whatever realm she was already in. He thought about the guy he'd met earlier who was making a killing in the real estate game. He thought about the credit card information he had on deck and what Venus could do with it; he even thought about Quesha, who had been on his mind a lot lately.

It was apparent, even though he tried to think about everything under the sun besides Li Chan's advances, that she was still able to arouse him. He figured he might as well fuck her one last time. Even though he hadn't fully worked out the plan, he knew he had a plan. The sun shone in through the kitchen window next to them, making Li Chan's skin look like ripe peaches. Key slid her robe off, letting it hit the ceramic tile on the floor. Li reached down and stroked his dick through his pants. She grew even more excited when she felt the length of Keyshawn's manhood.

He had a vision as she unzipped his pants. It was when he'd first fucked the only real bottom-bitch he'd ever have. The picture was clear to him as he enjoyed everything Quesha had done to him that day in her room. Li Chan was very pretty, but in his mind he exchanged faces, replacing her exquisite looks with that of his number-one money-getter. She inserted his dick in her mouth like an amateur and tried her best to make sure he was feeling pleasure. He played the part like she was the best as he tried to shove every inch down her throat and choke her to death right there just get it over with now. Somehow she adjusted and was able to handle all he was giving her.

Now he really grew excited, but stayed in character as he lifted her off her knees and turned her around. Keyshawn bent her over one of the kitchen chairs and entered her soaking wet pussy from the back. Li was tight; it felt like he was ripping her horizontally, but she loved every moment of the pain. He pulled her hair, snapping her neck back and pushing harder as she begged for more. The sweat beaded on his head, dripping as he mutilated her insides with his hardness.

Keyshawn couldn't remember feeling this much excitement in his life. He knew it wasn't excitement due to the actual nature of the act they were committing, but the excitement extended from him knowing one day she would no longer be a part of his future. No one he couldn't trust would be a part of his future.

Li Chan braced herself and backed steadily into him wanting more, covering his whole lower torso with her ass cheeks. Her body hungered for his attention sexually. She figured she had done so much to save him that she had won him over already mentally. Li didn't have the slightest idea Keyshawn had talked to his sister and found out Li had had her talk to Tiahmo right before she'd filled him with bullets. She was in heaven right now the way he was fucking her. If it was possible to get pregnant while already pregnant, she hoped like hell it was about to happen.

Keyshawn thrust several more pumps into her and felt her juices exploded all over him. He couldn't hold back as his juices left his body, and left them both shaking and exhausted.

"Damn, baby, you fucked me like you had a rough day at the office," Li said smiling.

"I sort of did," he replied, walking off and heading to the bathroom.

~ ❖ ~

SAIC Bender sat across from Agent Bennis, who looked like he'd lost several shades of coloring since they last time they were face-to-face. They kept going over the days he'd worked since the wire taps were introduced to evidence for safekeeping. Ex-Agent Bennis still bore a dumbfounded look; anything that had to do with evidence wasn't his department. Bender knew this but he wanted to be sure he could get a clear read on Bennis before he went into more strategic questioning. Things were exactly as Bender had thought; somehow Li Chan had used him to get his access code. Finding out how was going to be the trick. Bender was going to give Bennis a lie detector test, but he knew it would be useless. He could plainly see the man didn't have a criminal bone in his body.

"So, last week when you were at your station, you say the names on the list you provided were agents who had stopped and talked to you?" Bender asked.

"Yes, sir. I remember everyone who stops and speaks to me since not many field agents come down to the basement," Bennis replied.

Bender looked over the list and the only two names he was concerned about were Li Chan's and Daley's, her partner. It was a thought that maybe they were in on something together and it had backfired. Maybe that was what had gotten Daley eliminated from the equation. It was possible they both were on the take and they had both conspired to remove the evidence against Watson and Smith for a certain amount of currency.

Sometimes partners got close on the job and shared personal information no one else knew. Maybe, Bender thought, the looks Daley had been giving Li Chan were more than just looks. Thinking about the two sticky notes in his pockets, maybe Daley and Chan were fucking partners, literally. He knew if that was the case, something had to have gone terribly wrong, and the only one who could answer that was dead, thanks to Agent Li Chan who had tricked Bender into allowing her to go undercover on the spot. He was heated as he thought about the move she'd pulled to get inside the house with Daley's killer.

"Do you remember exactly what it was Agent Smith wanted when he visited your station?" Bender asked, not wanting to go right to Chan's and Daley's names.

"Yes, of course. He had a booklet from the dog track and asked me to look over the fifth race and pick a dog I thought would win," Bennis replied.

"So what happened?" Bender asked nonchalantly, remembering Agent Smith was a big gambler on the dogs and horses.

"I looked over the book like he asked; then I found a dog that should have been racing in a higher-class race and that was the one I picked."

"Do you remember the dog's name?" Bender asked, just making casual conversation before he moved on. He didn't care about a fucking greyhound any more than the man on the moon.

"If I'm not mistaken, it was *Unsung Hero,* coming out the eighth hole," Bennis replied. "The next day in fact, Smith came back to my desk and handed me a dozen chocolate chip cookies," he continued, trying to remember every detail just in case it would be of some help in restoring his job.

"I guess *Unsung Hero* crossed the finish line first," Bender replied, smiling. "Now you say Agent Daley also visited your desk that week?" Bender asked, getting to the nitty-gritty.

"Yes, he did. Daley was acting kind of weird though. He wanted to know what Agent Chan had just come to see me about. He said something about he was supposed to be out sick, and they were working on a case together and she thought he wasn't coming in," Bennis said, rubbing his chin.

Bender listened closely as Bennis talked.

"He said something about he'd missed her and she'd left her two-way on her desk."

"What did you tell him?" Bender asked.

"Well, the truth, I supposed. She wasn't really on much Bureau business, so there was nothing that could have tied into whatever case they were working."

"So what was Agent Chan working on?"

"She had me logon and look up something for her."

"Okay, that will be it for the day. Sorry to have kept you waiting for so long, but I was out on some important matters," Bender said, standing up.

"I hope I have been of some help, sir. I would love to come back to work soon."

"That just might happen," Bender replied, walking Bennis toward the door of the conference room.

Bender went in his office, sat behind his desk to think, and leaned back in his chair. If Daley was there questioning what Chan was up to, did he really know? Or was he just looking out for the double-cross? Bender removed the two sticky notes from his pocket and laid them on his light fixture. It was hard to profile one of his own. They were trained well and knew exactly what to do and not to do. He'd always thought, if he'd become a criminal, he would have been one of the best with the knowledge he had. But that was something the world never had to worry about.

The ringing of his phone jarred him out of his thinking process. It was his assistant. Bender looked at his watch and figured she should have been gone almost an hour ago.

"Yes, Mary; what's going on? No bridge game tonight?" he asked, wondering why she was still there.

"Yes, sir, we are meeting at one of the ladies' homes to play. Actually, I'm late, but there was something that was bothering me," she replied.

"What's that?"

"You had a call from an inmate at the House of Correction; he said he had some information on the Watson case that might be helpful."

SAIC Bender had dealt with informants before, and in his opinion, most of the ones he'd visited who were locked up usually had a bunch of he-say/she-say shit already known to him and his agents. People would do and say anything to be free of confinement. He thought about the last time he'd gone and seen a guy that was locked up in Waupun. This inmate claimed to have had information about a serial killer who'd buried bodies under vacant houses in the inner city. It turned out the guy was just making up stuff because he was once in the same cell with the guy they'd already caught.

It was a formality for the Bureau to still look into any calls that came through with the promise of information. Bender figured he would have Agent Love head out to Franklin to see the man in the morning. His mind was too tied up; right now he was preoccupied with trying to figure out the connection between Chan and Daley. He knew they'd each played a part, but he had to figure out what it was.

"Thanks, Mary; now get to your game. I'll check out this information first thing in the a.m.," Bender said.

"Not a problem, boss. Make sure you get some rest; you sound tired," she replied before disconnecting the call.

Bender knew that Mary was right in her assumption. He was extremely exhausted; tired was actually an understatement as far as he was concerned. Bender knew his body and mind were beat dealing with the Watson case. This whole ordeal had worn him completely down.

Agent Love decided to stop back at the mental complex to check on the patient Paris. He had been looking for any clues that could lead him to Li Chan's whereabouts, but he continued running into dead ends. Maybe he would talk to Bender in the morning and start following Watson. Even though his attorney had filed an injunction with the courts stating they weren't to harass Keyshawn Watson, a tail didn't necessarily mean they were breaking the law.

He pulled in the parking lot and removed his gun, putting it inside a lockbox between the seats. There was no need in setting off the metal detectors in the hospital. He would basically go in, speak to the doctor, and look in on the patient. It was a shot in the dark she would come out of her condition, based on what the doctor had said and filed in his last report.

Love wondered how a man could stoop so low and be so cruel to another human being. All his life growing up he was a fat kid who was bullied in school. He remembered one boy in particular named George Herman, who use to take his lunch money right before school every morning. When he got in middle school, there was Charles Bridges, who would hit him in the back of the head all the time and call him Rerun from the show *What's Happening*. He grew up hating that show. Then his first year in high school, he went out for football and a girl named Shunda Gleason had laughed at him when he fell trying to run the hundred-yard dash.

It wasn't until he switched schools and joined a military boys school that he started to find his way, getting into shape and becoming a decent-looking man. That school taught him character and integrity, and in his senior year, he took accelerated criminal justice courses, earning college credits. Love wanted nothing more in his life than to have authority over people like Charles, Shunda, and George. People like them were the scum of the earth, and Keyshawn Watson fell right in line with the three bandits he wished he'd seen today. He would file cases for harassment on all of them.

Agent Love walked through the front door straight to the counter to ask for Paris' doctor. The receptionist looked at his badge and summoned for the doctor to come up front. Agent Love checked his cell and saw he had somehow missed a call from Bender. It was after-hours, so he would just call him back after he left the visit. A few seconds later, the doctor walked up and both men shook hands like they were long-time friends.

"How's our patient doing, doc?" Love asked.

"I checked on her before dinner and she was still in the same state of mind. Her physical condition seems to have gotten a little worst though," he stated.

"What do you mean?" Love asked.

"She seems to be coming down with a touch of Vertigo, her blood pressure shot through the roof, and her heart rate was skittering off the charts."

"May I look in on her?" Love asked.

He knew it was a lost cause to get her to testify. The case was set for a speedy trial, but he knew there would be no trial without any hardcore evidence against Watson.

"Sure, be my guest," the doc replied.

Agent Love followed the doctor through a padded hallway that reeked of bleach and ammonia. The smell was so strong it was making Love a little dizzy. *'Vertigo my ass,'* he thought as he tried to hold his breath for five seconds at a time, pacing behind the doc. They came to the room Paris was supposed to be in.

"See, you can take a look for yourself, agent. She isn't going anywhere," the doc said, moving the sliding glass so Agent Love could see in.

"Nowhere, huh? Then where is she?" Love asked, looking at an empty bed.

The doc couldn't believe it. He unlocked the door and went in. Paris' nightgown was on the floor and there was a splatter of blood. They search the room, and when Agent Love went into the bathroom and pulled the shower curtain back, he found one of the second-shift nurses lying in the shower, naked.

"Doc, quick! Get in here!" he shouted. The doc came running, seeing one of his co-workers knocked out cold with a gash in her head.

"Is she dead, doc?" Love asked.

He checked her pulse, and luckily, she still had one. "No, she isn't dead, but I need to get her to ICU right away."

Agent Love got back in his unmarked and sat there for a second. He wondered what-in-the-hell had happened. If the girl Paris was in such bad condition, she couldn't have possibly escaped from the complex without help. He picked up his phone and dialed the one person he dreaded to call. He knew Bender was going to lose his fucking mind when he got wind of the latest development.

~ ❖ ~

Keyshawn had just come from seeing his lawyer and discussing their next move. T.A. was going to court tomorrow to take a plea for less time. They'd discussed T.A.'s decision and Keyshawn knew, whatever was transpiring, T.A. was most-likely making the best move. The lawyer explained the evidence they had against Keyshawn was really weak. He felt the U.S. attorney was either hiding something or stalling for time to find another person to testify against Keyshawn. His words made Keyshawn think heavily about that possibility, and if so, who could he find.

He thought about one person who could and would possibly attempt to do him in; that was Paris. But she was locked down in a mental facility and he had word her condition was permanent. Venus and Chrissy were both on his team until the end. Chrissy had pulled a foul move and she would be dealt with, but as for what he felt in his heart, she wouldn't go against the grain. He just wasn't going to take any chances.

Key reached in his jacket pocket and gave his lawyer twenty-five hundred dollars as the last payment. He knew he needed another ten bands if they were going to trial, which wasn't a problem. He had the money put up, along with a lot more, if needed.

"Make sure you stay clean, Mr. Watson, until this case is over with. I'm sure they're watching you despite the injunction," his attorney pleaded.

"Fuck them people! I haven't broken the law in the first place. They can watch all they want!" Keyshawn said, standing to walk out.

He got back in his rental and looked at the time. It was just starting to get dark outside, and he wanted to see his mother and sister before he hit the club to meet Bone and Bone's homie. He checked his rearview for the first seven blocks and was sure he wasn't being tailed, but he knew his attorney was right. They probably would soon be tailing him.

Key listened to *All Eyes On Me* as he hit the highway heading to the north side of town. For some reason, he couldn't get that boy Keith off his mind and the numbers he was doing with the real estate game. That was some serious paper to be making, and what was good about it was the law couldn't take a person down for selling and buying a piece of property. He felt it was just another form a pimping, but legalized pimping. He was selling property now—pussy was property without a deed.

He smiled at the thought of loving his occupation but Keyshawn Watson wasn't a fool. Coming up under T.A. and Big Daddy had taught him a lot of things. Besides, if Big Daddy trusted Keith enough to introduce them, there was something good about the nigga.

Keyshawn pulled in front of his mother's home and sat for a second. The song switched to *America's Most Wanted*, and Pac came right out with his gritty intro—*Ain't nothing but a gangsta party*. That was just how Keyshawn felt about him and T.A. They had put two of America's most-wanted in this bitch-ass city at the same time. He also had a quick premonition about his other brother Red; with so much going on and so many falling around him, he knew he would definitely call Keith sooner than later.

He got out the car and checked his surroundings. Everything seemed to be cool, and he proceeded to go inside to see the only two people left in the world he truly loved.

~ ❖ ~

Paris looked at the meter and saw it was already at twenty-five dollars. She didn't have any cash with her, but the driver saw she was wearing a nurse's uniform and didn't think twice when he pulled up in the bad neighborhood.

Somehow the medication they had given her had worked a miracle, and she was back to normal. She remembered leaving the casino with a man on a date and ending up in a hotel room where she was going to service him and rob him for the Rolex watch his wearing. Something went wrong and she'd blacked out. All she could remember after that was yesterday. The effects of whatever he had done to her had finally worn off. Paris wasn't a fool by a long shot. She knew deep down in her heart Keyshawn had been the one to set her up. He was livid she'd gone and talked to her ex, and wanted to prove she was in violation. His biggest mistake was not killing her.

The meter was at thirty dollars when the cab stopped in front of the house she'd given the address to. "One second; I don't carry cash, sir. Let me run in and grab your money and tip," she said, seeing the driver lick his lips when she said tip.

"No problem, ma'am. I just hope when I get sick, I have someone as pretty as you to make me feel better."

He was typical, Paris thought. Men always use the little head to think with instead of the one that had a brain. She'd done what she could to make herself look presentable, but she was nowhere near feeling pretty. She still had a bad case of the bubble guts and her hair wasn't combed at all.

"Okay; one second," she said, exiting the cab calmly, like she really lived in the building she was entering.

Paris walked up to the multi-unit and prayed someone buzzed her in. She rang all twenty-four bells at one time, knowing someone would be too busy to ask who it was and would just hit the buzzer.

Luck was on her side; after hearing several people ask who it was, finally someone buzzed her in. She looked over her shoulder, smiled at the cab driver, and put up a finger like she would be right back.

Once inside the building, Paris made her way to the back exit and down an alley, never seeing the cab driver again. She had one place she could go. There was her cousin Bella that Keyshawn or no one knew about. Bella was a Catholic nun and the two of them had once been close before Paris had chosen to give her life to the streets.

She ran through several yards, making her way over a few blocks, then hitching a ride with an old man in a van. All he wanted to talk about during the ride was how his medical benefits were all screwed up. She thanked the man when he pulled up in front of her cousin Bella's house and gave him a fake phone number. He smiled with two missing front teeth and said he would call her soon.

Paris walked to the front door of Bella's house, hoping she was home. When she rang the bell, she was shocked to see a small child come to the door. She hadn't seen Bella in four years and the child looked to be about the same age. When the little boy opened the door, she could see he looked exactly like Bella.

"Hello, is Bella home?" she asked.

The little boy turned and ran screaming, "MOMMA, THERE'S SOMEONE HERE FROM THE HOSPITAL!"

A tear started to form in Paris' eye. She had missed her life, but revenge was still in her heart. Keyshawn Watson had to be taught a lesson and she had to be the one to teach it to him. She had no idea what her plan was going to be, but right now she needed to get to a bathroom because the vomit was coating her tongue and on its way up.

Chapter 16 ~

Li Chan was in bliss. She was the happiest she had ever been in her personal life. She no longer cared if her family disowned her. Her only thought was about the new family she was preparing to make. Her life was all about Keyshawn and the little Keyshawn she was carrying. She knew wholeheartedly no one would ever understand the unexpected circumstances that consumed her, but she didn't give a flying fuck. It was her life and she had to live it her own way.

Li thought about all the men she'd once worked with and their infatuation with her beauty. She knew all they'd wanted from her was a piece of ass. Playing the role of Kimmie had really made her see things in a different light. It was the first time she'd ever gotten a chance to be on the inside and look out. Keyshawn was different. He was a pimp but she hoped the newfound love they shared would jar him away from that career and he'd go a different direction. Maybe having a son would help him choose a different life. Most men when they had children wanted a better life for their seed than they'd had. It still didn't matter to Li Chan. It was going to be whatever Keyshawn wanted.

She had hoped like hell she could keep the fact she'd involved Keysha in what happen with Tiahmo under wraps forever. That could never come to the surface. She sat on the couch in the Fox Point condo, drinking a cup of green tea and watching television. It had been a couple days since she'd been outside the house and she wanted to get some fresh air. Bender crossed her mind and she knew him well. He was a smart agent and would soon piece everything together that had happened, but none of that mattered. Li Chan had covered all her tracks thoroughly, and by time Bender was the wiser, she hoped to have talked Keyshawn into moving out the country.

They could move to Japan and live forever without anyone tracing their whereabouts. It was beautiful there with lots of opportunities for them to own a business. Of course she would convince him to marry her. That sounded good to her, Li Watson. It had a nice ring to it as she let the name roll off her tongue.

Li showered and dressed in a long sundress and a pair of Channel sandals she'd bought with some of the slush fund. The day was falling and the sun had disappeared, letting the darkness take over. The air was getting a little chilly, but she wanted to feel the breeze engulf her body through her dress as she got out and took a short walk.

Keyshawn pulled up to the club just as it was starting to get crowded. There were several reserved parking spots right up front for VIP guests. One for him and the other two were previously reserved for Red and T.A. He knew Big Daddy was left with no choice and would soon slot those spaces to someone else who spent out-of-control currency in his joint. Keyshawn saw the black Lincoln Town Car parked there as well, right next to Big Daddy's Bentley—the same car that was in the lot the day he'd met the real estate nigga Keith Swinson, who he liked. Key looked over to the right in Bone's parking spot and saw his main man's car was there.

Key sat behind the wheel thinking for a quick second. He had to do what he had to do in the midst of all the drama surrounding him. There was no other way to go about it, not if he was to ensure his own safety and keep his run in the streets going. He was still a pimp. He was either going to pimp or die, and death wasn't ready for a nigga like him—not in a face-to-face battle anyway—so the alternative was he had to pimp until he met up with death.

He stepped outside the rental car and moved quickly through the long line of patrons waiting their turn to get inside the packed club. It was jumping, but when Tommy and John-John saw him, they made the crowd part to one side so he could ease right on through. A few of the street cats who thought they were hard, or maybe felt they should have been considered elite clientele, gave Key a cold stare, wondering how-in-the-fuck he was able to move past them when they were willing to pay double the door charge. Key didn't pay any of the slick comments any attention like he would have normally. Instead of checking the suckas who fat-mouthed, he knew he was there on something far more important than what the little so-called D-boys looking to bang a bitch were on.

Soon as he stepped in the club, he saw a few familiar faces of some people who frequented him and his brother's club. He had to admit he'd missed the club scene as an owner. It had come with a lot of perks he wouldn't mind being exposed to again. Even though they'd been available, most nights, Key had passed them up. But keeping it real, there was a few times he'd wanted to get down with some of the bad-bitches who were willing to throw themselves at him and his niggas just to be privy to a drink and the right to say they'd fucked a playa. But since none of them wanted to put in work like his ready-made stable, they'd ended up not being his cup of tea.

He spotted his man by the ohhh's and ahhh's surrounding the pool table. Bone was doing his usual thing, running the crap game and trimming the fools for their paper. Key walked over to where the game was taking place and just watched for a second, smiling, knowing Bone was the luckiest, if not the best, nigga he'd seen shake a pair of dice.

"Bet a G, I make my point," Bone said to some little nigga draped in silver-colored chains that hung down to his belt.

"A fucking G, nigga? That's it, big homie? I wipe my ass with hundreds, nigga. Bet this money if you can stand it," the little nigga replied, throwing down a wad of bills that looked to be three-to-four racks.

"You nooooo-money-getting-ass nigga," Bone said with overeager eyes. "Bet that money. I can put that shit in my daughter's piggy bank," Bone continued, shaking the dice and rolling them out halfway down the table.

"Come on, hoes; let's welcome this poot-butt nigga to the cheesecake factory," Bone called out as the dice both stopped on trays, pairing up to equal six.

Bone's point was six, and when the dice registered, he saw the nigga's face frown up. Bone wasn't worried about foul play; mad or not, it didn't stop him from raking in the bet the lil homie had just placed.

"I'll be back, little nigga; hope you've got something left in them parachute-ass pants you're wearing, looking like Turbo from *Breakin'*," Bone continued, shitting on the lil homie as he stashed the money in his blue jean pockets.

"Damn, my nigga, you going to win one bet and hit it on a nigga like that? Shit! Then you talk real slick to a nigga while breaking 'em, huh," the little homie said, going in his side pocket on his leg and pulling out a knot twice the size of what he'd just wagered.

"See, if they keep printing this shit, I'm going to have it before the ink dries," he continued talking, being a little wise nigga himself.

"I got some business to handle fo' a sec, lil nigga. Just don't lose it all before I get back. I know your momma told you bear meat is sweet," Bone replied, walking off with Keyshawn.

"Fo' real, my nigga; you jumped a point on a nigga and talked that slick. That's why I don't fuck around with them gamblers, homie.

Shit, a nigga like me, I'd be wanting my shit back," Key said, making sure they were out of ear range from the game.

"Listen, playa," Bone said, "I told you this gambling shit is sweet as momma's apple pie, nigga. You think I'm playing fair with these sucka-ass nigga's?" Bone asked.

"What you mean?" Key asked.

"I got magnets under that muthafucka, and look over to the right." Bone nodded in the direction of a square-looking nigga who appeared to be chasing pussy. "That's my nigga Cory. He's got the trigger button, nigga. I'm never going to miss my point, not for that type of money," Bone confessed.

"Shit, well I see you've got your niche going, homie," Keyshawn said. "Have you heard from your man yet about that other business I needed to be on?" Keyshawn asked, wanting to get the ball rolling.

"Have I? Listen, big homie, my people don't play. When it comes to making that loot, they're ready to get on their grind."

"That's cool; I feel that."

Key followed Bone to the back of the club, waving off this thick-ass redbone who tried to get in his business. He had seen her the last night they were open for business at his club. She had some thick thighs and was nice on the eyes, but she wanted him on some sucka-shit and he wasn't going. Keyshawn and Bone took a seat at a table where a dude was sitting by himself. The cat had on dark shades and an all-black Dickie suit, with the shirt buttoned all the way up to the neck. Key took one look at the homie, and knew as hot as it was in the club, he had to be a crazy muthafucka to be in there kited up like a Rican.

"Key, meet my nigga Ed; some people call him the Torch. Ed, meet Key," Bone said.

Both men exchanged glances before extending a hand to make the meet-and-greet formal.

"Well, I'm going to let you niggas handle y'alls business. I've got to get at mine," Bone said, heading back to the pool table to scam the little homie for the rest of his bread.

"I heard your resume is a beast, homie," Key said, not really liking talking to a man wearing dark shades.

Ed smiled, his teeth were all white except one of them in the front, which was platinum with a round, stone diamond mounted in it. "Let's just say I do what I'm paid to do—nothing more, nothing less."

They were just about to start talking when Keith and Big Daddy walked up. "Neph, hey, I didn't see you come in. You remember my man, Keith?" Big Daddy said.

"Hey, Key; what it do, brother? Still waiting on that phone call; got some sweet deals that came across my desk this morning," Keith said.

"Yeah, man, I've been giving that shit some real thought, too. I think I'm going to be calling you real soon," Keyshawn replied.

"Now that's what I like to hear; we going to own this city."

The same redbone who was at Keyshawn was on his arm now. She followed Keith to the private VIP suite in the back. Key smiled at her and turned his attention back to Ed.

"So now that we're back to business, I would like to hear what it is you want me to make my business."

"Murder, homie; I need some people ten-toes-up," Key replied steely-eyed. Keyshawn watched when he said what he needed to see if the dude across from him would tense up any.

Ed removed his shades for the first time. He was a slight man in his thirties who bore a dangerous look on his face. His eyes were smoldering but domineering. He definitely had a look that could kill, if nothing else.

"See, now we're talking my language. I don't understand anything else but murder and money. The rest of that shit sounds French to me." He smiled.

Keyshawn took three photos out of his pocket. He looked at each one of them, placing the photo of Li Chan back in his pocket. He wanted to add her to the list, but figured he might have to hold out on her for a second. He thought about the baby inside her and wondered if he could actually kill his unborn child.

He passed Ed the first photo of Chrissy. He knew she was no longer an asset but a liability. She'd jeopardized him by pulling that little stunt at the mall and blatantly going against his orders.

"Here's the address where you can find her. There are going to be two women in the house, but the other one is to be untouched," Keyshawn said, making sure Ed was clear not to harm Venus.

"As you wish; you're the boss," Ed replied.

Keyshawn then gave him a photo of Paris and told Ed she was in Mendota. He asked Ed if that was an issue.

"Listen, homie, the bitch could be at a meeting in the oval office and it wouldn't make a difference," he replied with no dissuasion to his tone.

This was the moment of truth for Keyshawn. He was now playing chess and going for the checkmate. Every victory had come down to a serious singleness of purpose. He was resetting the board and moving the pawns around to protect himself, the king. He felt an adrenaline surge as he handed Ed the Torch an envelope with twenty-five thousand in it. Ed took a look at the green inside and was ready to commit the obscene act of homicide.

"I'll make contact through Bone; consider the job as good as done," Ed said.

Keyshawn stood to shake his hand but it was too late. Ed was already making his way to the door to handle his business. Keyshawn walked back over to where the dice game was taking place. He looked at Cory, who was Bone's man, and he looked as innocent as a politician at a bunny ranch. Their scheme seemed to be working out just fine; Bone had about twenty thousand in front of him now.

~ ❖ ~

Paris sat in the living room on the couch; her cousin Bella had finally put her son to bed. She waited with a look of astonished disgust plastered over her face. She knew her life had taken the turn it had because of the choices she'd made. Paris had come from a good family who'd tried their best to keep her from hanging in the inner city with the people they'd called scums and low lifes. But the more her father tried to keep her from seeing black men, the more curious she'd become.

She had no idea the first one she would open her legs for was the one she would fall in love with. That was exactly what had happened. When she had finally met Keyshawn, leaving her ex alone because of the violence he bestowed on her, she'd thought she'd died and gone to heaven. Her ex had made her familiar with fucking men for money, so she was comfortable with that part of it; what she didn't like were the beatings he would put on her when he felt she was short, or if she'd spent money on food or pads.

Keyshawn was totally different. He was gentle and soothing, and sometimes when he opened his mouth, she would think he spoke better than the great Edgar Allen Poe himself. She had begged Keyshawn to make love to her, and for some reason, he'd always told her now wasn't the time for that. They had to reach a goal, then he would make love to her like nobody's business. It hadn't mattered to Paris. He had taken such good care of her, she would do anything Keyshawn had asked her to do. It was the little unscheduled adventure of the new bitches that had made her weary and grow tired of what had been happening.

Finding out Key had fucked Venus was a little too much for her to deal with. Paris knew she was wrong for contacting her ex-pimp and using that as an excuse. She had been taught well by Keyshawn and her wife-in-laws that trying to run off to be with another daddy was considered the ultimate betrayal, but Keyshawn had to realize she was only human. How was he going to fuck one of his wives and not all of them? Or at least her? Paris felt she looked better than every one of her coworkers, and if her daddy needed a night of relief, she should have been the chosen one. She'd really had no intentions on leaving once she walked out, but she felt like she needed to teach him a lesson to see if he would sweat.

Bella came and sat down next to her cousin. She put her hand on her lap and told her the Lord was going to watch over her. They talked a little about Bella's life and how she'd gotten pregnant and left the convent to live a life of a mother. Paris knew Bella had known what she was into. She loved Bella the most out of everyone in her family because Bella had never judged her. She didn't even want to go into great detail about where Paris had been or what had happened to her. Paris was cool with that because she didn't want to explain either. She wanted revenge for what Keyshawn had done to her. He'd tried to permanently ruin her life and she wanted to do the same to him now.

Her cousin gave her a blanket so she could lie down and get some rest after she'd showered. Paris hugged and thanked Bella for all she'd done for her. She watched her cousin walk off to go lay it down for the night. The hot shower felt good as the water soothed her skin. Paris had been through so much, and it had gotten worse because she'd had to fake her condition the last three days in the hospital, plotting her escape. Now she was out of that place, she could plan on getting back at Keyshawn. She dried off and made a pallet, lying down on the floor in front of the sofa. Surprisingly, she drifted right off.

Chapter 17 ~

Agent Love decided to go home and get settled, instead of calling the boss. Soon as he sat down with his favorites—Twinkies and a glass of chocolate milk—his cell began to ring. He wanted to watch the episode of *Law and Order Special Victims Unit* in peace and not be disturbed. He looked at the caller display and see it was SAIC Bender calling him.

"Good evening, boss."

"I was waiting for you to check in, Love. What was the outcome?" Bender asked, getting right down to business.

"I actually just made it in. I didn't get any leads on Li Chan again today, so I went out by the hospital and attempted to check on the girl out there," Love replied, a little hesitant. He knew Bender was going to let him have it when he find out he hadn't reported something as serious as a disappearing mental patient.

"Attempted? Well, exactly how does one *attempt* to check on a mental patient?" Bender asked.

"Well, boss, I said it that way because she wasn't there. We found a nurse in her room, hit over the head with some type of blunt object and naked. The girl must have taken her clothes and run off."

"WHAT IN TARNATION?!" he screamed. "And you weren't going to call me on this?"

"Of course, I was going to call you; like I said, I just walked in. The locals are there on the scene waiting to get a statement from the nurse when she comes to."

"I need to see you first thing in the morning in my office. Better yet, I need you first to go out to the House of Corrections and take a statement from a possible informant claiming to have information on Watson. Let's see if you can at least get this simple task right!" Bender said, hanging up and disconnecting the call.

There was nothing Love hated more than to be treated like an incompetent person. He knew his job well. In fact, if there wasn't so much politics involved, he felt he was a better fit for the head of the department than his boss was. Bender was an overeager hotshot who didn't know his own asshole from a hole in the ground. Love opened the box of treats and stuffed several Twinkies down his throat. He turned the volume up on his television and listened to the opening of his favorite police show. He thought maybe one day he could be the voice that introduced the show, leave all this chasing real bad guys to the jerks like Bender. He had made his mark in life.

Bender sat on his bed thinking he was losing control of the situation. Every time he turned around something new was surfacing and working against him. Not that he was banking on any information from the mental patient, but the fact that she'd gone missing didn't help at all. The papers would report it and he would look even dumber than he was already looking thus far.

He lay down but couldn't sleep. All he could do was stare at the ceiling and try to put the pieces of what was going on together. Watson wouldn't be dumb enough to go to the hospital to try to get the girl out of there, and if he had, what would he want with her? None of his other girls were giving any information against him, so why would he risk going for this particular one?

Something Love had said made Bender think it wasn't Watson at all. He'd said the nurse had been stripped of her clothing—only a woman would do that. Paris had to have escaped from the hospital on her own, he thought.

"But why?" Bender said out loud, causing his wife to turn over in her sleep. Bender rose up. "That's it!" he said.

"Honey, what's it? Why don't you get some sleep?" his wife said, mad he'd awakened her for the millionth time.

He always did his best thinking in bed. He thought about having a twin-size bed placed in his office to lie on to think, but the Bureau wouldn't approve it. Keyshawn had to be responsible for the condition the woman was in. It was too coincidental she was slipped something right in the middle of their investigation. He was sewing up loose ends, Bender thought, and Li Chan had to be his accomplice, helping him to beat the system. Bender was finally able to get some rest. He turned toward his wife, pressing his shaft up against her backside.

"Oh no you don't, buddy. I have an early hair appointment in the morning," she said, knowing exactly what her husband was up to.

Bender didn't mind. He just closed his eyes and went to sleep. He had some things he had to attend to in the morning.

BOOK THREE ~
MOTIVATING MOMENTS

Chapter 18 ~

The dark-colored mini-van pulled up to the address on back of the picture Keyshawn had given him. Ed the Torch looked at the face one more time before sticking the photo back in his back pocket, thinking how sweet it was going to be to smell the searing skin of Chrissy. Killing for him was second nature, and there was nothing more than taking a life he loved besides eating fast food.

He reached behind him on the back seat of his fully-loaded Town and Country mini-van, and removed his weapon bag containing all his special tools. Ed knew he could have easily used a gun and blown her brains out, but he hated loud noises. He actually couldn't wait to get out of the nightclub where Bone had had him meet Keyshawn. With the loud music blaring through the huge speakers, it was giving him a migraine headache; pain was something else he hated. He only liked heat; he wasn't called the Torch for nothing.

Edward Amos, Jr. thought about the first time he'd ever killed. He was eleven years old and his neighbor had a nerve-wracking dog that barked all through the night, disturbing him while he looked at his father's dirty magazines. Every time he would try to go to sleep with visions of naked women, the dog would go at it, barking for hours, giving him pain inside his head.

He decided, as he listened to the mangy mutt drone, it would be its last night interrupting him and his thoughts. Ed took several of his mother's light bulbs, unscrewed the bottoms off, and filled them with Kingsford lighter fluid. Ed went in the kitchen and stole a pork chop to use as bait. Still in his pajamas, he took several rags and went out the back door through the yard where the dog was in his cage. He watched as the dog became silent, mauling the pork chop like it was the best thing he'd ever had in its menial life.

As he tied the first cloth around the bulb and lit the end, he licked his lips at the sight of watching the noisemaker's life come to an end. Seconds later, the smell of burning fur and animal flesh excited him as he continued breaking the bulbs, sending the dog to its timely death. That was his first kill and something about death intrigued him immensely. Ed took a break, and when he turned eighteen, he gave himself the best birthday a deranged person could receive—his first body.

It had been ten years. His body count ranged in the high numbers and he'd managed to stay off any law official's radar. Ed exited his van, thinking he was a little upset his new boss had said he had to leave a person alive. That wasn't his normal skilo. He didn't like to leave anyone behind, but her destiny was going to be on her. Once he set the place ablaze, she was responsible for her own escape.

He walked around to the back of the building, jarring the door, which had a cheap lock. It was easy as one-two-three for him to get in. It was late, and he expected them both to be sleeping as he heard the soft music coming from the front of the house. Ed walked through, looking at the neatly-furnished place, and admired the taste the women had. It was a shame all that expensive furnishing would be ashes in the next twenty minutes, but business was business.

He walked by the first bedroom and looked in on the sleeping beauty. She was curled up, naked on top of her sheets, exposing her goodies for the world to see. Her caramel skin color and thick round ass told him she wasn't the girl on the picture. He took another look, feeling a rise inside his pants, wishing that was Venus. Ed would've liked to have fun with her before he ended her life.

The next bedroom was far enough away that he could do his thing and not wake the beautiful one who was sound asleep in the other room. When he got to Chrissy's door, Ed heard a television going.

He also heard snoring and figured she must have fallen asleep watching something on TV.

When he cracked the door making sure she was alone, he saw her well-put-together frame. She was also lying naked in her bed, just like her roommate had been. Chrissy's pale skin was flawless, unmarked, and ready to bear his signature as he crept in and stood over her body. He was a master at creepy and moving ninja-like when he did his thing. Chrissy had a nice set of titties and her blonde her was long, matching the small patch neatly manicured between her legs.

The Torch sat his bag down and went to work right away. He removed a thin roll of wiring he liked to use when tying people up. It was very sharp and would cut through the skin of a person whenever they tried to move like they wanted to get loose. He slowly bound Chrissy's thin wrists, using military knots, to each of the bedposts.

When Chrissy tossed and turned, the pain ripped through her body, almost feeling like she'd just been electrocuted by a million volts. She opened her eyes and was shocked to be peering in the ugliest face she had ever seen standing over her. Once she attempted to scream, the Torch stuffed a rag filled with a foreign substance deep down her throat. Fear filled her eyes, but she was rendered helpless, wondering what fate the cards had dealt her.

Ed went to work right away, removing a sharp carving knife from his bag. When Chrissy saw what the scary-looking man had in his hand, her eyes grew wide as they could go. The solution on the rag was starting to take effect and she was slowing losing consciousness, but not before she felt the first incision from the perpetrator's knife behind her left ear. Blood gushed, landing on the nose of Ed the Torch.

Before he commenced doing what he did, he stopped and tasted her blood. The taste of the red liquid fueled him as he began slashing her until her life slipped away from her. He had a sad look on his face that lasted only a second before his grin took over. Ed took the gasoline from his bag and doused her body and entire room with the flammable fluid. He bent down over her when he'd finished packing his tools, kissed her on her thin lips, and told her dead body, "Maybe in another life we could have been lovers."

Ed walked to the door, making a trail of gas behind him. Once he got to the entrance, he looked back at his work one more time then lit the match. The room was instantly engulfed in flames and the same smell he always remembered from his first kill filled the air. He made his way out as the smoke detectors went off, alarming anyone else who needed to escape.

Ed made it outside and sat in his van for a few seconds, watching the blaze illuminate the neighborhood. He saw the other girl, Venus, safely escape the burning blaze. She ran out screaming for help, wrapped in a comforter, protecting her body from the growing crowds that had begun to emerge.

Edward Amos turned the key in the ignition and let his engine purr to life as he headed toward the freeway. He was ready to make it to his next destination and earn his money. Ed knew he would be at the hospital where his second victim was supposedly waiting in about fifteen minutes. The vision of setting an entire hospital on fire made his dick hard as he smiled entering the on-ramp.

Keyshawn hit the highway, headed back out to the Fox Point Condo where Li Chan was waiting for him. He thought about the conversation he'd had before leaving the club with Keith Swinson. Key was actually amazed at how knowledgeable the man was when it came to investing money and making what you had grow into some real currency. Keyshawn had made his mind up he was going to do business with the man as soon as his case was over. If Big Daddy trusted the dude, there had to be something good to it. Big Daddy was surely nobody's fool.

Key's next thought was about the other man he'd had a conversation with earlier—the crazy-looking dude who called himself Ed the Torch. Ed seemed to be just what he needed to replace his homeboy Tiahmo. There was something really sinister about the man Keyshawn liked. He wondered as he looked at the speedometer to check his speed which of the girls he would take care of first. When Ed explained how he made sure the bodies were almost unrecognizable, it seemed to be a highlight for him. It didn't matter one bit what his fetish was to Keyshawn; he just wanted the job done and done correctly.

Thinking back on when he'd first got in the game, Keyshawn knew it wasn't going to be all peaches and cream. Only a sucka thought that way, and that was why they made so many mistakes. He told himself when he first got down, he would never be a sucka and would handle his business like a player, a real man, at all times. He knew he had a down-ass click of down-ass bitches who were real ride-or-die whores.

He also felt the love he shared with T.A. was real brotherly love. He knew from being in the streets all his life that not many men got a chance to vibe with niggas who had the same goal in mind as they had. Most were faced with jealousy and envy from their immediate circle, making it hard to know who to trust and who not to trust; so most didn't trust anybody at all. Since most niggas in the street never trusted anybody period, a man could be in your face cleaning his knife, talking some real shit, and as soon as you turned your back, that same knife was clipping your spinal cord. It was serious in a hustler's world.

It was different for him, Red, and T.A. They had come up together as kids, and right from the very beginning of them meeting each other, the bond they had built with one another was very strong. Even when he'd left to go down south to stay for a while, Keyshawn had known with those two he was never forgotten, not by his true homies.

When he pulled off the freeway and into the condo's parking lot, he found an open spot next to Li Chan's car. Keyshawn killed the ignition and just sat there for a few seconds to meditate on a few things. He really couldn't remember the last time he'd shed a tear over anything, but as so much drama had flashed on him, a few fell from his eyes. Death seemed like it had become a part of his life now and seemed to be plaguing him every chance it had to do so.

It had all started in New Orleans with losing his bottom-bitch to a sucka. The nigga was so shiesty and wasn't man enough to get at Keyshawn, but had tried to hurt him in the worst way. The killer part was he'd actually succeeded because her death had hurt him badly, but losing his brother to a bullet had hurt him even more. He knew they weren't on their P's and Q's when they got caught slipping, and they'd paid the price. Red had paid with his life and Key had paid with his heart. Revenge felt sweet but still, even though they merc'd them nigga's, it wouldn't bring Red back.

Now that Keyshawn's true feelings had surfaced for his father, he felt he'd never really hated his father deep down inside. He understood he'd just despised the man Tim had turned out to be. Thinking about Tim was the only reason he'd held back from giving Ed the picture and address to the Fox Point condo to eliminate Li Chan. He knew, if it wasn't for the unborn child she was carrying that he'd fathered, he would have had her done first for betraying him and involving Keysha in her scheme. He knew she felt she was doing what was best, but to him his family had no business in his business like that. It was too risky and he wouldn't be able to live with himself if Keysha or his mother went to jail, or something bad happened to either of them.

The life of a player was truly hard. It was a dirty game, and Keyshawn had to make each and every move with caution. Otherwise, just like many men before him, he would be the bearer of a big downfall. Keyshawn knew he had to hold things down, not only for him and his family, but for T.A., who was counting on him as well.

He went inside and saw his future baby-mama lying on the couch covered in a Japanese kimono. She had fallen asleep drinking her third cup of tea, trying to wait on his arrival. Keyshawn stared for a moment, but didn't bother to wake Li Chan, knowing he didn't really want to talk to her right now. Hearing her voice would make him regret not going through with his first mind. He knew, if his baby wasn't in her stomach, she would be dead right now—nothing left to tie him into anything since she'd disposed of all the evidence that could convict him. It was still a thought, but he would have to make other arrangements for her, knowing he couldn't kill his baby and his mother's only grandchild. Li Chan was lucky she was still breathing. He looked at her one more time, then simply went into the bedroom, closed the door behind him, and fell asleep.

Chapter 19 ~

Keysha decided to go visit Brandon early again today since she had some things she needed to do later. She needed to be around in the afternoon to go shopping with Michele for birthday gifts for her grandmother in Mississippi, so she hoped Brandon wasn't all sweaty again from playing ball in the gym when she got there like last time. It was sexy, but she couldn't get to him and that bothered her.

The line at the House of Corrections was longer today than normal. It was like it was Fathers' Day or something. There seemed to be more ghetto chicks with extra-extended ponytails waiting to see their loved ones than normal. When Keysha got up to the front desk to show her ID and give the name of the inmate she was there to see, the guard looked at her funny and told her to step aside for a second. The desk guard said a superior officer was on the way down to speak with her.

Keysha was a little nervous, thinking maybe something bad had happened to her man. She was going to go off on the guards if Brandon had been jumped by any of the crazy criminals in there, or if he had broken a leg playing basketball and they hadn't called her to let her know. Keysha's name was the first name on his contact list to call in case of an emergency, so by law, they should have informed her of any medical mishap first. She stood aside, watching the other girlfriends enter the visiting section one by one carrying babies and diaper bags on their shoulders.

She waited impatiently trying not to get herself too worked up until she found out exactly what was going on with Brandon. It seemed like forever, although it had only taken about ten minutes before an overweight, truculent woman appeared, wearing a white shirt with a gold badge matted above the left pocket.

"Ms. Watson, can you please step over here with me for a second?" the fat commanding officer said in a mean tone.

Keysha was worried all over again. Now she had to be talked to in private. It wasn't looking good as she walked behind the woman. "What's this all about?" Keysha asked, speaking first because she was concerned.

"Well, Ms. Watson," the woman said, looking at Brandon's rotor card, "I'm sorry to inform you Brandon has lost his visiting privileges for the rest of his stay here. Your boyfriend was found this morning to be in possession of a cell phone. Normally, we would add another charge, but since he has had nothing but good behavior and no other problems, he isn't going to be charged with uncontrolled contraband in a controlled rea at this point," the woman stated like she was doing Keysha a favor.

"So will he be allowed to use the regular phone?"

"I'm afraid not at this point. He's being kept in solitary confinement, which could last about thirty days, maybe sixty, depending on the officer who holds his final hearing. When he completes his hold time, I assure you he will be released back to general population."

Keysha was ready to cry after she heard what was happening. She had just lost all communication with Brandon, and he was in solitary confinement, which she figured had to be hard on him.

"Ah, there is one other thing, Ms. Watson," she said, staring at Keysha.

"What is the one other thing?"

"Whoever's number is on the call log will be restricted when he is released," she said, turning and walking away.

Keysha knew she was probably the only person Brandon was talking to besides his coach, who was like a father to him. So not only could he not call her or she come see him for the remainder of his stay in jail, but even after his punishment they still wouldn't be able to talk. She felt that the system was dishing out cruel and unusual punishment.

At this point, there was nothing Keysha could do but turn and walk away herself. She left through the same doors she'd come through, now teary-eyed. First thing she did when she got back in her car was she attempted to call Keyshawn. Key always knew what to say at times like these to make her at least feel somewhat better. She dialed his number but the phone went to voicemail. When she tried the second time, she got the same results. Keysha felt like the world was crashing down on her. It was going to be a very long six months without Brandon.

Agent Love saw the teary-eyed young lady leaving, figuring she'd had a terrible visit. He'd just walked right past Keysha Watson, not even knowing the teary-eyed woman was the sister of Keyshawn Watson. He entered the House of Corrections on the federal business his boss, SAIC Bender, had sent him to handle.

Bender had called him about an hour ago and informed him he'd had the dorm where Brandon was housed shaken down, and the latest thing he'd heard from the captain out there was Brandon had been taken to the hole for contraband. Brandon was not directly involved in the Watson case as far as Love knew, but the informant had extracted the information he was about to give because of him, and Bender wanted to keep things cool until he found out what was what. Love knew exactly what his boss was doing.

Agent Love knew the Feds first priority was to protect the informant; once they got whatever they needed from the person who'd given up the voluntary information, they were done. The system had changed from the old days, when alleged suspects were able to find informant's names given in their discovery. The Feds now recorded every thing on digital recorders, only giving informants' numbers when it was time to go to court. It was ordered of the Government in a supreme ruling, in attempts to make it seem they were at least trying to protect the snitches who were joining forces with the authorities.

Agent Love showed his credentials to the same front-desk guard who had shown Keysha out. The guard quickly summoned the white shirt in charge back down to her station. Agent Love didn't have to wait as long as Keysha had for the fat woman. The same commanding officer appeared almost instantly when the call came across her radio in code the Feds were in the lobby.

The white shirt escorted Agent Love to a private room where the visitors coming in on visits wouldn't be able to see him or who he was talking to, another safety precaution. She made small talk with Agent Love like she'd once in her menial life actually had a chance to join the FBI and chase down real criminals. Different branches of law enforcement always looked to be better than the other, like one job was more important than the other and carried more weight. Being a babysitter at the House of Corrections didn't even meet the ranks of law enforcement as far as Love was concerned. Agent Love just looked at her size and knew she was telling a lie. The oversized Krispy Kreme customer didn't have a chance in hell of becoming an agent with the Bureau.

It only took a few more minutes to get the man in front of him who was supposed to have pertinent information ready to be divulged about Keyshawn Watson's case. Love could see him being escorted in his orange get up, and could tell at first sight the man was a bona fide tattle-teller. Once Jamal sat down, they both began to size each other up—Love getting a read on him, and Jamal seeing if he was going to be played by the system. Agent Love actually hated snitches, but he couldn't reveal that to Jamal or to his boss. It was really how the conviction rate stayed so high. Informants took a lot of footwork out of the job for people like Love.

"Do I need to have my lawyer present?" Jamal asked.

"Why would you need a lawyer? Did you do anything wrong?" Love questioned back.

"Come on, man. Don't try to play bad cop/good cop, and you're the only one here. I got some shit to say that I feel I should be freed for," Jamal said. "I don't just go around giving information freely. I got another year in this place and I don't want to do it if I don't have to."

"Well, you must be going to give us the addresses to where the rest of the Al Qaeda crew is staying." Love replied, fucking with Jamal's emotions.

"Shit, I'm going to tell you what happened to that dead Fed y'all found in the park," he said, watching Agent Love for a reaction.

"You seem real familiar with the law here," Love said, "so you know I have to take whatever you tell me back to my boss and the information has to thoroughly check out. I take it you already also know something of this magnitude will go to the State's Attorney on your behalf," Love continued, trying to make sure he confused Jamal.

"So I would have to sit and wait on the State to make a decision, huh? Some cracker decides to give me a reduction or not? That shit could take months," Jamal replied, knowing exactly how it worked. It wasn't his first time off the porch. He had told on someone before and gotten himself out of jail before the booking paperwork was even entered in the system.

"Listen man, we just don't go turning the jailhouse cell keys, letting bad people walk out of places because they gave us some information. There's a damn procedure to everything. Now we can get this ball rolling, or you can sit your time out back upstairs and we will nail this clown anyway. Furthermore," Love stated, "if I find out you're wasting my time and got me all the way out here in cow milking land on a wild-goose chase with some jailhouse shenanigans, I swear you're going to wish you hadn't called our office," Love continued with finality in his tone.

Jamal had snitched before, but it was only to the local police. He had never dealt on the federal level and figured the Fed meant business. He was instantly shaken up by Love's threat.

Agent Love removed a tape recorder, sat it in front of his man now, then looked Jamal in the eye before speaking. "Are we ready now?"

Jamal nodded his head up and down, signaling yes to let Agent Love know they could begin. Jamal had made it a point to get as close to Brandon that night when he was on the phone talking to Keysha and that was when he heard him discussing in detail what had happened.

"This is Agent Brian Love with the Federal Bureau of Investigation. My badge number is 23321. I'm currently sitting in Franklin, Wisconsin, with informant number 132, ready to discuss said relevant information regarding the Keyshawn Watson case. Informant is giving information on his own free will with no promises made from myself or anyone else from the Federal Bureau of Investigation," Love said, sitting the recorder back down in front of Jamal a little closer, so everything Jamal was about to say would be clear.

~ ~

Outside the Franklin Facility Agent Love almost lost the contents in his stomach as he replayed the information on the recorder. Jamal didn't know everything, but being a good agent, it was easy for Love to piece together what had gone down. It was a shame one of his old crushes had turned to the wrong side of the law. The sad part was she'd jumped the fence so hard, she'd even had her own partner killed.

Agent Love removed his cell from the glove box as he started the unmarked unit. He was about to make the phone call to SAIC Bender, who he knew was going to blow his lid clean off. Bender would put every man on the force out there to find Agent Li Chan after Love shared what he knew. That would serve her right for being such a tight ass all those years. She'd never looked his way; now she was going to spend years in a prison and probably get the chair for her involvement in the death of her partner.

Chapter 20 ~

Ed the Torch had struck out at the hospital last night. He didn't have a problem getting in through the service doors, posing as one of the cleanup crew. He'd pushed the yellow mop bucket around four floors looking for the girl on the photo. It wasn't until he went into a break room where there were several nurses taking a late, third-shift break.

He continued to sweep, mop, and wipe down the vending machines acting as if he wasn't paying attention. He got his break when a fresh-faced blonde walked in discussing the escape of a patient who'd bashed her coworker over the head. The girl wouldn't stop talking about what had happened since she'd been forced to come in on her day off.

Ed smiled at the ladies and placed his mop back in the bucket, leaving behind a yellow caution, slippery when wet sign. He didn't really have any idea now where to find his second victim since she wasn't where she was supposed to be. What he liked was knowing Paris was a fighter and she would probably resist him trying to take her last breath from her.

Leaving back out the same way he'd come in, Ed the Torch climbed back in the driver's seat of his mini-van. He took out the picture of Paris again, wanting to see her beautiful face. When he was done admiring the astonishingly dashing bone structure, he put the picture close to his own face and kissed her on the lips.

Ed placed the photo over the driver-side visor and started humming the melody to *Where Oh Where Can My Baby Be*. He changed the next measure to fit his A-type personality. '*She left the hospital and went away from me.*' He smiled again as he let the visor down and took one more look at Paris' face. He knew he might as well enjoy it for now because it wasn't going to look like that once he found her and did his thing. Ed knew one thing was for certain: Paris could run, but she couldn't hide. At least not from him; it was his city and he could actually find a needle in a haystack if he had to.

~ ❖ ~

Keyshawn smelled the aroma from the breakfast as he turned over in the bed. He had seen the pillows next to him were ruffled and not like they were when he'd fallen asleep. He knew at some point Li Chan had gotten in the bed. He wondered if she'd slept or if she'd lain there watching him sleep. He got up because he knew she wasn't a great cook, but it smelled really good for some odd reason.

When he walked into the kitchen where she was, he noticed she had on a different kimono, one that was a little sexier than she'd had on last night. Key saw the pudginess in her stomach region and was for a second glad he'd changed his mind about giving the Torch her photo. As much as he wanted her to never be able to do him in, he wanted that child to be born. He thought about something his grandmother use to always say when he and Keysha were kids and lost their grandfather: usually when God's takes a life, He gives a life. Still not the biggest believer in all that, he felt it may have some validity with his father and Red dying. But his mind was made up; her flight was already booked for seven o'clock tonight.

When he was in the parking lot of the condo last night, before coming in, he'd phoned Venus and given her instructions on what to do and how to handle it. He figured using the information Li Chan had provided him with the credit cards, it was going to be untraceable. Venus said she'd found one name that sounded Japanese and that was what she was going to use. They both thought it was smart to book the international travel that way to reduce any suspicion Customs might have.

Venus was still distraught about what had happened with the fire, but Keyshawn knew she was smart. When he didn't come to see about her, she knew he had to be behind it. There was no need to question him, because if he'd wanted her dead, she knew she would have been dead. He'd waited on her text confirming the flight before he exited the car.

Now as he sat down at the kitchen table, it was time to break the news to Li Chan about his decision. He was a pimp and his job was to manipulate by means of finessing a bitch's mind. He wanted to see the baby and have his seed raised in America with him, but he had to work the plan he'd devised to make sure Li Chan went along with what he was going to lie and tell her was best.

"Are you hungry?" Li asked, placing a plate in front of Keyshawn.

"Yeah, it smells good. I thought you might have called in a chef or something," he replied smiling.

Keyshawn reached for the remote to turn on the flat screen TV that sat above the countertop. Li filled his plate with scrambled eggs, turkey bacon, and hash browns. He switched to Fox 6 News while she buttered the biscuits.

"Last night a woman was caught in a deadly fire at this north side residence. Her body was burned beyond recognition, but thanks to her roommate, she was identified right away. Her name is being withheld until further investigation by the local authorities are complete. We will be sure to keep you updated as reports come in. This is Jessica Rodgers reporting for Fox 6 News."

Li Chan almost dropped the flat pan of biscuits she was holding on the floor when she realized it was one of her friends who had been killed in the fire. She looked at Keyshawn and could see he already knew about it by the way he showed no emotion.

"So which one of the girls was it?" Li asked.

"It was Chrissy. Venus is okay and I had her moved to Chicago for safekeeping until I sort this mess out," Keyshawn replied.

"Damn, Chrissy was so young and beautiful. This can't be happening."

"Shit is real. My ears in the street are telling me there's a nice-size bounty on my head and all my people's heads. I got some people on their way into town to help me get to the bottom of this," he said, getting up and walking over to stand next to her. He could see the tears start to form in her eyes and was satisfied his plan was working so far. Keyshawn used his index finger and lifted Li's head so they made eye contact.

"What's wrong, Kimmie?" he said, using her street name; doing so on purpose. He wanted to look at her like she was a hoe. Even though she'd never sold a piece of pussy, she was still his bitch and he need to keep a reminder of that floating in his head.

"I can't even use my contacts to help because there are no more contacts. Hell, it's possible Bender has me on the most-wanted list by now," she said, wrapping her arms around him.

It was the right moment now. Li Chan was getting weak and Keyshawn knew best when to attack a hoe's inferior feelings.

"Keyshawn, I don't want anything to happen to you, myself, or this baby inside me."

"I know, baby girl; daddy understands that. Nothing is going to happen to either of you. I'm sending you back to Japan tonight," he said, kissing her.

Li backed her lips off his, making sure she had just heard what he'd said.

"You're doing what?" she asked.

"Listen, don't ever question me again! You're carrying my child, and if something happens to that baby over this shit, I wouldn't like it. So I know what's best for you!" he snapped.

"I'm sorry, daddy, but for how long? How am I going to know you're safe?" she asked.

"Listen, this isn't about me or you. It's about the baby, so I think with all the trouble that's going on and you retiring, this gives us a chance to see what's really up. You will be safe over there and my child will be safe. I will come to Japan as soon as the baby is born," he said, telling the truth about that. Keyshawn knew he was going to go to Japan to bring her and the baby back; then he would give Ed the other picture he'd held onto.

"Okay, daddy; if that's what you feel is best, we don't have a choice," she replied.

"I need you packed and ready by five. We need to be at the airport two hours early," he said, walking off to go shower and hit the streets.

Chapter 21 ~

Paris didn't want to steal her cousin's car, but she didn't look at it like she was stealing. She figured she'd borrow Bella's car, handle her business, then return it before she caught a cab to the train station and made her way to New Orleans to start her own escort service. She had stopped at the Bus Stop Café on 45th and Lisbon since it was still early and it was the only place she could think of to get a cup of coffee and a banana chocolate chip muffin.

She was sitting at a small table by the window when the morning newsbreak came on. They flashed a picture of her friend Chrissy and said the woman had been killed by a fire. It was all starting to make sense to her now. Keyshawn was trying to rid himself of anyone who might bring harm to him. Paris knew Chrissy worshipped the ground Key walked on and wondered why he'd had this done to her. The news lady mentioned a roommate who'd made it out alive and that could only be Venus. Paris knew Keyshawn had knocked up Kimmie and she would be somewhere else, separate from the other two.

It was a shame everything had come to this. All she'd ever wanted her whole life was to be loved by a man, any man. It wasn't her destiny to become what she'd become, but the cards had dealt her a hand and she played it. Now sucked into the life, she wasn't going to fold. Paris felt her revenge wasn't only going to be for her, but for her good friend Chrissy as well. Keyshawn Watson had gone too far.

Paris entered the phone number on her cell and dialed Venus. Venus had no idea Keyshawn was responsible for what had happened to Paris. There were some things he talked about and others he felt were just on a need-to-know basis with any of the girls. Venus answered the strange number thinking it might have been Key calling her. Lately he had been changing phones to be safe.

"Hello."

"Hey, girl; what's going on?" Paris asked, keeping it cool to see if she could get a read on her. Paris knew Venus was in line to become the next queen, or the bottom-bitch, so she had to make sure to see if Venus knew Keyshawn was responsible for her being drugged.

"Paris? Is that you, sista?" Venus asked, surprised to hear the voice.

"Yes, it is me."

"Girl, what the fuck? I heard you were in some mental hospital because shit went wrong on your last date!" Venus exclaimed.

Paris could hear the sincerity in Venus voice and knew that she was none the wiser. "Yes, I'm getting better now. I was sitting in my room when I saw the news flash about what happened."

"I can't believe it either. Chrissy was a trip, but she was my girl, you know. I didn't want anything bad to happen to her. This doesn't make sense though. I still don't understand how she left a blunt burning and started her room on fire," Venus said.

Paris had a notion Chrissy didn't leave a blunt burning; Keyshawn had had her killed. "So what in the hell happened over there?" Paris asked, needing more information.

"Keyshawn had her on room confinement because she did something he'd asked her not to do." Venus explained.

Venus told Chrissy all about the mall incident and how mad Keyshawn was about it. Paris knew that was what had gotten her friend killed. The Feds were on to Keyshawn so he wouldn't want to take any chances. Paris knew that was how he operated.

"Is Kimmie okay? I didn't see anything about her on the news," Paris pried even deeper.

"Yeah, girl, her pregnant ass is fine. I'm glad she's leaving this bitch today. I like her, but I think Japan is a better place for her," Venus said.

"What do you mean, Japan?"

"I booked her muthafuckin ticket to go home. She's out of this bitch at seven tonight. I'm so glad you're feeling better. I can't wait for you to come home. It's going to be just me, you, and Keyshawn for a while."

"Girl, this doctor is calling me for meds. I'm going to call you back. Don't tell Keyshawn I called. I'm going to surprise him with a call tonight around eight when they let us out our rooms for social rehabilitation time."

"Okay, sis; you take care of yourself in there, and if there's anything you need—panties, bra, some real food—don't hesitate to call me," Venus said, ending the call.

Paris started to shed tears about the death of her friend Chrissy. She soaked the top of her muffin and didn't want it any more. She sat there thinking for a while, and knew as soon as her thoughts were completed, what it was she was going to do. She needed to hit the hood for a gun.

SAIC Bender decided not to go home last night. He knew after hearing everything Agent Love had to say he wouldn't be able to sleep. His wife preferred on nights like that, that he didn't come home and interrupt her. He woke up on the small leather sofa in his office, still in shock that Li Chan had gone to the extent she had gone.

Bender was upset he'd let her play him during the hostage situation, but admired her for her courage to even try it. He now knew she'd shot Tiahmo to keep him quiet. Li Chan was also responsible for her own partner's death. After looking back over the sticky notes that were attached to Daley's refrigerator, Bender decided to try to figure out what the acronym S.W.A.L.B.A.K.W.S. meant. He surfed the Internet and couldn't find anything until he scrolled all the way done and a database for urban writers popped up with a link. Bender found out the term was used by an urban writer in a police crime drama novel called *Cricket and Honey* and it meant, sealed with a lick because a kiss won't stick.

It was all coming to him now—the surveillance equipment and the little innuendos on sticky paper. Daley was in love and had found out Li Chan was playing both sides. Bender figured he'd either tried to reason with her, or he tried to blackmail her. The reason part he figured had gone out the window with Daley when he found out Li Chan was carrying the child of a criminal. Bender figured Daley had lost all respect for her, but love had made him not turn her in. So he blackmailed her for money and her walking papers from the Bureau. Well, it was obvious he'd gotten one of the two.

It all started to come to Bender when he'd last interviewed Agent Bennis, who he knew he would give his job back. Agents were supposed to trust agents, not think they were up to anything. Bender knew Li Chan had tricked Bennis out of his logon, watching him enter it into the system. She'd done so to demolish the wiretaps that would be used to send her baby-daddy away for a long time.

What Bender wasn't sure of was what Li Chan was thinking. How did she figure she was going to get away with doing what she'd done and not get caught? Killing Tiahmo, a good lawyer might have beat that and gotten Internal Affairs to lift the charges, but killing one of her own was punishable by death. Bender took Li Chan for a smart agent, not someone who would fall in love with a man like Keyshawn Watson, a person who manipulated women into selling their bodies for personal profit.

He sat at his computer, yawning and finishing up the APB that would go out nationwide to all law enforcement agencies. He thought, *'There is no place in the United States she was going to be able to hide.'* Then it hit him plain as day. *"United States? This girl is going to make a run for it."* He knew Li Chan was going to leave the country. She could easily go back to Japan and never be discovered.

Bender picked up his landline and called out to a man he knew well. Agent Roy Jimmerson was in control of what the Bureau called travel agents. They were the group who patrolled the bus stations, train stations, and the airports. He knew he needed extra men at Mitchell Field; Li Chan was going to make a break for it.

Chapter 22 ~

Ed the Torch had done a little research on the missing patient Paris, and found out her only relative left in Milwaukee was a first cousin named Bella Jenkins. He used his contact at the Water Department to find out where Bella Jenkins' bill was being sent. There were two Bella Jenkins in the system, and he knew which one it was because one of them was ninety years old.

It was close to four o' clock when Ed pulled up at the address he was given by his friend. The Torch was always prepared; he was dressed in an outfit like he worked for the Water Department. He was glad there was a fire hydrant outside to make his spiel easier. He went to Bella's door, and when she answered, he explained there was a water leak in the main sewer line. He needed to check her basement for leaks. Bella saw his badge and didn't hesitate to let the man in. The last thing she needed to hear was she was going to have to file a claim with State Farm for a flooded basement.

Ed was thinking how sweet it was to get a freebie in. He was going to kill Bella just because she was in the wrong place at the wrong time. He just needed a clue to find out where Paris might be. When he came out the basement, Bella was in the kitchen, standing with her son who looked just like her. The little boy ran up to Ed asking to see one of his wrenches from his tool belt.

Bella looked at Ed and said, "He was always infatuated with tools."

"He is a darling," Ed replied. Bella didn't know her life had just been saved.

"Hey, do you have a garage? I need to check one more thing," Ed asked.

"Yes, that door right there. Go ahead; it's empty. My cousin was by here and stole my car. I swear that girl is always in something."

That was what Ed needed to hear. Now he knew Paris was mobile. He faked a search in the garage with his flashlight with Bella's son by his side. "Well, there are no water spots here, young man," he said, smiling at the child. The little boy ran in the house screaming there were no water spots in the garage. His mom scooped him up as Ed reentered the kitchen.

"Everything looks good here. You say your cousin stole your car? Man, that's got to be crazy," Ed said, seeing if he could get more info from her.

"Tell me about it. It's just an old Camry, nothing to cry over, but I did call and report it," she replied.

"Still sad," Ed said, knowing he was getting somewhere. "You know I had an old Camry. I called mine the gold creation because that thing ran forever. I had over two hundred thousand miles on it."

"Mine is a 2000; funny though, I call her blue bonnet," Bella replied, not knowing she'd given Ed everything he needed to find Paris.

Keyshawn had just ended his call with Venus, letting her know everything was going to be all right. They had sentenced T.A. to fifteen years earlier that morning and Keyshawn was hurt by the length of time, but he knew T.A. would probably give back half the time when his appeal came up. Key was still a little worried about his day in court that was coming up soon. He knew they didn't have much on him, but that didn't mean anything when the Feds were involved.

He got out the car and went inside to grab Li Chan and her bags. Keyshawn hadn't heard anything about Paris and hoped Ed had handled his responsibility. Inside, Li Chan was sitting on the couch holding a picture of him. Tears were flowing from her eyes as he watched her put the picture inside her Coach purse.

"Ain't no time for crying. We've got to get you out of here," Key said, still standing on her hard.

"I know, baby, but I feel like my life is over," she replied.

"Listen, Li, if I didn't love you, this wouldn't be a problem. I need you and need for you to be safe," Keyshawn said lying, making her warm up a little. He couldn't wait to get her on the plane and in the sky. They packed the car and hit the highway, heading toward the airport interchange.

Agent Love was riding up Locust Street, ready to hit the highway and head back to the office to meet with Bender. They were supposed to be setting up a manhunt to track down Li Chan, and bring her and Keyshawn Watson to justice. He was at a traffic light on the corner of Locust and Teutonia when he saw a dark-blue Camry whiz past him. When he saw the face behind the wheel, he was stunned. He picked up his two-way and called Bender. Bender told him to trail her and find out where she was going. He was wondering if she was going to lead them to Watson and Chan.

On the side of Love was a Town and Country mini-van that had seen the same thing Agent Love had seen. Both cars simultaneously made U-turns to follow the Camry. Ed the Torch had no idea the other car was a federal agent in pursuit of his girl. He took the picture of Paris from his top pocket and smiled. "Yes, I told you, honey: you can run, but you can't hide," he said to himself. He turned up the volume on the radio as he gingerly stayed a of couple car lengths behind her.

Agent Love used his cell this time to call the boss. He told Bender it looked like she was heading toward Mitchell Field Airport. Bender told his man he was on his way. When they ended the call, the first thing he did was call Jimmerson to put his people on high alert. He figured, if Paris was heading there, she was trying to make a break for it. Not that it made sense to Bender because they actually didn't have anything on her, but her trying to run showed guilt and maybe they could get her to talk. Just maybe, she would reveal where Watson and Chan were hiding.

Key pulled the rental up to concourse C, where Li Chan had to catch her flight. He was held up by the long line of traffic waiting for parking spots—some waiting for passengers that had just landed, others dropping off passengers and saying their goodbyes. A sheriff was coming through making people hurry up, so Key went around one more time in hopes of finding a spot when he returned.

This time he was in luck. Two spots opened up right in front of Delta and Southwest, and he dipped the rental curbside. He reached in the glove box and hit the trunk latch before he turned on the hazard lights.

"You know I'm going to miss you, baby," Li said.

He didn't want to start with all this lovey-dovey-ass bullshit. It was time to get her out of Milwaukee, but one last motion wasn't going to hurt. He reached over and kissed her softly on the lips.

"Look, Kimmie, we both know this is best. If we're going to have a family one day, this is how shit has to be for now," he replied.

"I know; doesn't mean I have to like it;" she replied.

They both got out, neither paying attention to the dark-blue Camry that had pulled a couple parking spots behind them. Paris was observing them through the Gucci shades she'd found hanging from the rearview mirror. It was time for her to get her sweet revenge, removing the nine millimeter from the center console she'd bought from some lil homies in the hood.

Li Chan stood on the platform while Key started getting her bags together. The five o'clock air started to chill her neck a little and she closed her coat. She wondered how her family was going to take it when she arrived expecting a child. That wasn't so bad, but expecting and not married was going to be what set them off. She had visions of their child, how pretty the baby was going to be. She'd seen pictures of some of the women from her country who'd had babies by the African American men in the military. They always had the prettiest babies she'd ever seen.

"Grab that cart, baby girl," Key said to Li, pointing at the empty cart he was going to use to carry her bags.

The airport Feds were searching all over for Paris or anyone who looked like her. Bender had texted a picture to Jimmerson, who'd sent it to his people to be on the lookout. Agent Love had pulled behind Paris and was wondering why she hadn't got out yet. He wondered if she was on the phone talking to either Chan or Watson. That was when he looked ahead and saw both the people he was also looking for. He hurried and dialed Bender's phone again.

"Yeah, what you got?" Bender said, answering as he floored his unmarked with twelve other units in pursuit with him.

"Boss, I just spotted Watson and Chan as well. They're all here," Love replied.

"Okay; I just passed the Lincoln/Beecher exit. My ETA is about five minutes. Just keep a watch on them. You already have backup on site."

"Not a problem, sir. Wait; Paris is on the move," Love said.

"Okay, follow her. I'll radio Jimmerson where you are."

Ed the Torch saw Paris on the move. He wondered how he was going to play it in such a high-security area. Going inside the airport was pointless. If she made it to the second floor and got to the boarding area, he would never be able to get her. He rummaged in the back of his van looking for what he needed. "There you are," he said to his trusty flamethrower. His John Deere, gas-powered, four-stroke flamethrower could send out over three hundred ninety degrees at six-feet. It was perfect if he hurried and got her before she went inside.

Li Chan dropped her purse and the picture she had of Key had fallen out. She was still bent down wiping it off, when she heard a familiar voice.

"So you two are taking a vacation, I see," Paris said, standing in front of her, pointing the gun. Key was busy with his head bent down, grabbing the last bag, but he heard all the screaming and tire screeching, and wondered what was going on. When he looked up, he almost lost his mind. He was standing there looking at Paris, who was supposed to be dead.

"Paris, what the fuck are you doing here?" he asked.

"Nigga, please! You thought it was going to be this easy? You killed my nigga Chrissy, tried to strip me of my mind, and you've got this bitch knocked up. You just thought I was going to let you fly off to Japan and eat fried rice for the rest of your life?" Paris replied.

"Bitch, you must lost your fucking mind fo' real! We're in a damn airport! You are crazy! That jealousy is what fucked you up, not me."

Key saw a familiar, ugly face behind her, approaching with something in his hand. There was only one mug shot like that in the world.

"Well, call it want you want. I was diagnosed as crazy anyway, so when I kill you and this slant-eye freak, I'll spend a few years in the crazy home and be free as a bird to run my own escort service," she said.

Li Chan was trying to edge a little bit closer so she could disarm Paris. She was thinking she could catch her with a flying kick to the face and retrieve the gun. When she looked over Paris' right shoulder, she saw a man starting some type of gadget that looked like a leaf blower. But that wasn't what startled her. Agent Love, one of her ex-coworkers, was walking at a fast pace right behind the man. When Li Chan made up her mind to make her move, the sound was so loud it echoed on the platform, it sounded like a plane had crashed. The bullet hit her in the chest, sending her tumbling backwards and landing face down in a pool of blood.

Agent Love had drawn his gun now. He was aiming for Paris, yelling FBI, but the sudden burst of light and heat stopped everyone in their tracks. Paris didn't what had happened as she felt her skin begin to melt. The second gunshot went off and Ed the Torch fell forward as the bullet opened his head up like a cantaloupe.

The ambulance medics tried to save Li Chan, but there was no hope. Bender stood next to the gurney as her life slipped away from her. Keyshawn was placed in the back of one of the unmarked units and told he was under arrest.

Epilogue

Three days later, the cell doors opened. Keyshawn walked out and was escorted to the property room. Bender was pissed. He had spent seventy-two hours trying to get the Grand Jury to indict him for everything from tampering with a federal investigation to accessory to the crime of murder. There were no witnesses left to testify against Keyshawn Watson. His old suit had come through again and filed a motion to have him immediately released from custody. The judge had no choice but to grant the motion.

Bender stood behind a glass watching Keyshawn Watson dress back in the blood-stained clothes he'd been wearing. He had held Li Chan in his arms, crying, after Paris had shot her. It wasn't for her he'd shed tears; it was because his unborn child wouldn't live to see the light of day. Key heard the agent unlock the steel door that separated the inside world from the real world, and once on the other side, he was free to go. When he stepped in the hallway, SAIC Bender and Agent Love were standing there.

"The law will catch up with you, Watson. I'm sure we'll see you again. Next time you won't be so lucky," Bender said.

Keyshawn didn't reply to what Bender had said. He stepped outside onto the Federal Courthouse steps and saw the black limousine waiting. Venus got out and opened his door, holding a glass of champagne in her hand. When Keyshawn got inside, he shook hands with the one man who had been on his mind for the last seventy-two hours.

"You ready to do this shit now, young playa?" Keith said.

"I'm going to tell you like this," Keyshawn said, throwing his arm around Venus as she put the glass to his lips, "if it don't make money, it don't make sense."

~ ❖ ~

Three months later ~

Keyshawn hugged Big Daddy in front of a waiting crowd. His first investment with the three hundred thousand Venus had stolen using the credit card info Li Chan had given him had gone to good use. She'd taken a chance. She knew she was either going to end up like everyone else or end up the bottom-bitch for life. It had taken her forty-eight hours to formulate wire transfers into fake accounts and remove the money. She had talked to Keyshawn's lawyer and knew he was getting out, and all the charges would be dropped. She figured she had to do what a hoe had to do to make sure her daddy ate well when he came home. She had no idea they would be married, and she would be carrying her daddy's first baby.

"Cut the tape! What you waiting for?" Keith said.

"This is Milwaukee, man. It's cold as fuck out here!" Big Daddy said. They all laughed.

"You know what? I think I'm going to let my bit—, I mean wife, do the honors," Key replied.

He looked at Keysha and Brandon standing there, and Brandon gave him the thumbs up. Keyshawn passed Venus the scissors, and she cut the red tape that meant Allure 2 was open for business. The waiting patrons all screamed, for the opening night was ladies' night.

Keyshawn looked up to the sky and said his first prayer.

ORDER FORM

Book Series

-BARGAINS RATES -
PURCHASE ANY 2 BOOKS FOR ONLY $20.00
PURCHASE THE ENTIRE MOTIVATION BOOK
SERIES FOR ONLY $28.00!!

Quantity	Book Title	Cost	Total
	MOTIVATION MASTERING THE GAME	$11.99	
	MOTIVATION II THE CHASE	$12.99	
	MOTIVATION III THE EXIT	$14.99	
	VIA U.S. PRIORITY MAIL S/H $2.99 FIRST BOOK $1.00 EA ADDITIONAL BOOK WISCONSIN RESIDIENTS MUST ADD 5.6% SALES TAX		
	Total Submitted		

MAKE CHECK & MONEY ORDERS PAYABLE TO:
R.H. PUBLISHING, LLC P.O. BOX 11642 MILWAUKEE, WI 53211

Name_____

ID#_____

Institution Name_____

Address_____

City_____ State _____ Zip _____

FOR ONLINE ORDERS VISIT:
www.swiftnovels.com

Made in the USA
Monee, IL
11 July 2023

39048716R00108